E. A

Estate agency at its ~~best~~ worst...

A novella by Elizabeth Coffey

© Elizabeth Coffey 2019. All rights reserved

ELIZABETH COFFEY

A slice of village life...

CHAPTER ONE

*THE BISCUIT AND
THE ORANGE*

Nestling between the affluent suburb of Burkes End and the slum known as Marshfield, proudly stood the mediocre village of Waddley Bottom. Home to average folk, Café Olé, the Adam and Eve pub, a kebab hut, a Chinese takeaway, four Indian restaurants, oh and two rival estate agencies, one of which being Hardman and Camp.

CEO, Gary Hardman was on the phone to a car leasing company. "How much? For two BMW's?" He glanced across to his partner Nigel, and lowered his (ever so slightly camp) tone. "Haven't you got anything cheaper – how much? For a Ford? That's ridiculous – what's the cheapest?"

***

The Monday morning team meeting. Lisa was chewing gum, daydreaming out of the window. The rain was tipping down on the huge glass front of H&C making the place more boring than normal. As for her colleagues – she glanced around at them – equally boring.

There was Rodney Root-whatever-his-name-was, the antiquated office supervisor, with his permanent half-smiling-half-dumbfounded expression. Nigel Camp, the company co-founder/part-time comedian – leaning against the wall with his arms folded, trying to make his biceps look bigger than they actually were. Big boss (literally) overweight, effeminate, Gary, what a chump, standing in front of the nobo board with his hand poised in the air, in his pink shirt, ironed by his horrible-bitch wife. Beside him; new recruit, Lucy, fresh out of Cardiff Uni, desperate to impress in her flash designer suit. Give it a month, on these wages she'd be in ripped jeans like Lisa.

The trainee office creep was clearly suffering first day nerves, and good, it should help brighten things up a little.

"A big warm welcome to our new recruit, Lucy Ranus, she's recently moved to Burkes End all the way from Aber – is it wrist-witch?" quizzed Gary.

"No, wrist-watch," replied Nigel, in his gravelly cockney accent.

"All the way from Aberwristwatch." Gary smiled

confidently.

"It's Aberwrist*wyth* actually," said sheepish Lucy in her drawling Welsh accent.

"As you can see Nigel's our office joker." Gary rolled his eyes. "As I first said, Aberwrist-witch." He clapped, and everyone slowly joined in. "We now have a Lucy and a Lisa on board this tight ship, hmm, bit similar, we'll have to differentiate somehow."

"She can be posh Lucy 'cos she lives in Burkes End." Nigel belly-laughed.

"Good idea, Nige, and we'll call you poor Lisa." Gary pointed at Lisa.

"Why am I poor? That's so unfair," sulked Lisa.

"Because you're from Marshfield. Right everyone let's introduce Lucy to our code of ethics."

Gary looked around the room for inspiration. Office geek to-be, Lucy, thrust her hand into the air like a kid in a classroom. Gary looked at her, confused. "You don't know them yet."

Lucy blushed and put her arm down, much to Lisa's delight.

"Neither does that one," said Nigel, nodding towards Rodney.

"Code of ethics?" Gary continued. "What is it we never *ever* do – rubbish Lisa?"

"Excuse me? I'm poor thank you, not rubbish."

Gary turned his attention to office supervisor, Rodney.

"I've got no idea," said Rodney, half-smiling, half-dumbfounded.

"See, I told you," Nigel shrugged.

"No! Never be honest Rod!" Gary scowled. "If we don't know the answer?" he prompted.

Nigel and Lisa chanted in unison. "Make it up!"

"That's right, we don't want to look incompetent, if a house is falling down, what do we say? Tell her Nige."

Nigel stood up straight, with his arms folded across his chest, and adopted his best salesman act. "This place is full of character."

"Absolutely, ethical code number two – make it up, and what's the first, anyone?"

"Wow," said Lisa, in a bored tone.

"Well done Lisa, which means? Every-one?"

Everyone – Nigel and Lisa – answered in unison. "Never discuss work outside work."

Gary wrote 'work outside work' on the nobo board underlining the letters W. O. W.

"We have to remain professional at all times, everyone knows everyone around here posh Lucy, which means everyone is a potential customer, the golden and number one ethical code is, never discuss work outside work…"

Gary's voice trailed off, Lisa's attention started to wane, she squinted out of the window across the road to rival estate agency Brangwin & Ball. Cheeky Dan was eyeballing her through his office window, gesturing with his shirt for her to lift up her shirt. She mouthed the words *not now.* Gary's 'ahem' broke her out of fantasy land.

"As I was saying, Lisa, it can get you into heaps of trouble."

Nigel raised his eyebrows. "You'd know all about that wouldn't you Gary?"

Gary cut Nigel a look then turned his attention to Lucy. "Always remember WOW and you won't go wrong. We'll go through the rest later. Now then, I've got something new and exciting for everyone." He stuffed his chubby hand into a carrier bag and handed out name badges to all the staff. "Posh Lucy, I've given you full title on yours, it'll help with the whole Lucy, Lisa thing."

"There aint enough letters in the bag for Rodney Root-Vujasevic to have full title." Nigel laughed.

Lucy examined her wonky 'R' and attempted to straighten it.

"No, no, Lucy, don't fiddle." Gary smacked her hand lightly. "It'll fall off, bloody eBay, I've ordered more R's we should have them soon." He put on his badge re-adjusting his own crooked 'R'. "Right then, allow me to reveal our brand-new fleet of company vehicles." He led the team to the back door and opened it wide. "Tada!"

Parked side by side, in the empty car park, were two bright orange smart cars with the logo HARDMAN & CAMP. A dog cocked his leg against the wheel, peed and walked away. Lisa shot Nigel a sideways glance. He looked pissed off. She muffled a giggle as he stomped over to the solitary cars and peered through the window.

"I thought we agreed beamers!" he shouted over his shoulder. "I'm 6 foot 3 Gary, how the f –am I supposed to fit in that?"

"You can always," Gary mimicked opening a sunroof. "It is a convertible you know."

"And if it rains?" Nigel pointed to the darkening sky. "Seems our new fleet is not so *smart* is it, Gary! I'm off to do a viewing in a proper car." He stormed off, got into his BMW and wheel span out of the car park.

"Such a prankster." Gary grinned at his team and quickly closed the door. "Right, chop-chop, work to be done." He ushered everyone back to their desks. "Lisa look after Lucy, show her the kettle, the toilets and stuff, I'm off to Burkes End to win over Mr Buckley, unlike sulky Nigel, I will be using a company car we've got to impress him. Rod, you can use the other one until he puts his toys back in the pram."

"Thank you," said Rodney half-smiling, half-dumbfounded. "That's awfully kind, Gary."

Gary threw a set of keys onto Rodney's desk. "It's an improvement on that moped of yours."

"I'm not so sure," muttered Lisa.

"Pardon Lisa?" Gary eyed her questioningly.

"I said for sure!" she grinned like a Cheshire cat.

"Oh wow, you drive a moped Rodney?" asked Lucy.

"Yes I lost my licence," Rodney whistled through his teeth.

"What for? Drinking?"

"Good Lord no, I don't drink. I'm forgetful enough. No I lost it, literally."

"Then he sent off for another one and then he lost that," said Lisa, shaking her head.

"Then I thought: not much point getting another one. I've forgotten which pedal does what."

"I'll put stickers on each one Rod," said Gary. "A for accelerator, B brake, C clutch. Remember ABC and you'll be fine, don't want you crashing into a shop front again do we."

"Ooh, I nearly forgot, Gary," Lisa piped up. "Mr Buckley said can you meet him in his field, the entrance is off Love Lane. Hang on let me check the email."

Lisa opened the laptop and her phone rang. She plonked the laptop on Rodney's desk and nodded for him to check. He stared at the computer as if it was evil. Gary rushed over, picked up the laptop and plonked it back on Lisa's desk while she was chatting on the phone.

"I'll post them out today, thanks for the call Mrs Tyler, bye now." Lisa put the phone down and frowned at Gary. "Why can't he do emails? What's the point of him being here if he can't use a computer? Why have I got to do everything?"

"Lisa we've been through this time and time again. Rod doesn't like computers you know Rod doesn't like computers."

"Not fair." She pulled a face.

"Drop it, Lisa."

Lisa sighed. "Whatever Trevor." She scrolled through the emails but couldn't find it. Damn, she must have deleted it by mistake. *Private message* appeared in the corner of the screen, she clicked on it; *meet me by the bins in five*, it said.

"Sometime today, Lisa." Gary drummed his fingers on his desk.

"Mm? Oh sorry, yep, definitely says Love Lane," she answered, starry eyed.

"I'm off." Gary grabbed his coat. "If either of them

phone or call, remember the Buckley's are VIP's and the difference between us getting a bigger office or you lot being made redundant. We've got to get this deal if my brother gets it…"

***

"…I'll never hear the end of it!" Richard Hardman, MD of rival estate agents Brangwin and Ball, slammed his fist on the desk. "We've got to get this deal Dan, by fair means or foul, I've left a voice message inviting the Buckley's to pop in for coffee and a chat. He won't come but she will, and that's exactly what we want."

"How can you be sure?" asked Dan.

"A, she's a coffee-aholic, I've seen her, she goes in Café Olé every other day. And B, they're splitting up. She'll come. I'll charm the pants off her, we'll get the deal and live happily ever after, the end."

Dan rubbed his hands together. "A cunning plan."

"Intelligent prospecting, that's what it is," Richard winked. "Oh, seeing as you're so bloody good at disappearing acts *Dandini* make sure you do one when she comes in please."

Richard's attention was thwarted by the door-ding-a-ling. A wealthy looking blonde-haired female walked in and started browsing the property board.

"Dan, have I got any bits of fluff on my suit?" whispered Richard.

Dan eyed up Richards navy blue suit. "There's no fluff on your suit."

"Stray hairs?"

"No Richard, no stray hairs honest."

Richard smoothed down his suit and straightened his tie. He was tired today, that was the only reason his OCD was in overdrive. Nothing to do with the fact he was a merciless ladies man and she might be Mrs Buckley. He gave his wingman the signal to leave and sauntered over to the customer. Dandini slunk out the back door.

***

Dan was already waiting for Lisa in their regular spot, behind the shops by the wheelie bins. She raced over to him and they started snogging. Two minutes in, Dan's mobile shrieked *cock-a-doodle-doo* and they stopped kissing abruptly. Dan took his phone out of his pocket and turned the alarm off. He lit two cigarettes, gave one to Lisa, and they leant against the wall and started puffing.

"Crap! I think I forgot to shut Facebook!" Lisa exclaimed.

"No you didn't. You're just being para," Dan laughed.

Lisa was being para, and justifiably so. She and Dan had been secretly and madly in lust for just over a month now. Dan was Richard's loyal protégée, and Richard was not only Gary's (much better looking) younger brother, but also his arch rival. Gary was a stickler for loyalty – ethical code number five. If he found out about their fling, she'd be out of a job, hundred percent. Not that she liked her job, but being a single parent she needed the money. Lisa took a few extra-long puffs, trod her cigarette out, kissed Dan on the cheek, he pinched her bum and off they went, back to their respective estate agencies.

Lisa straightened her pony tail, put a chewing gum in her mouth and walked casually back into the office to find posh Lucy nosing at her computer.

"What do you think you're doing?"

"I was looking at your computer," replied a startled Lucy.

"I can see that," Lisa tutted. "Why?"

"Gary told me to familiarise myself with what you do, and I um – noticed something."

"What did you notice? Facebook?" Lisa dared to ask, colour rushing into her cheeks.

"No, I was checking emails, Mr Buckley said meet him by the entrance to the field, not *in* the field, like you told Gary."

"Is that it?" Lisa let out a sigh of relief. "Field, entrance, entrance, field, whatever Trevor, Gary's a big boy he'll work it out."

Lucy blushed.

***

It was pouring with rain as Gary drove tentatively into the mucky field. He opened the car door and stepped his polished shoe straight into deep mud. He cursed, retracted his foot, shut the door then realised he had no shoe on. Cursing again, he opened the door, retrieved his shoe from the squelchy mud, shook it, and put it back on. He rammed the car into reverse, gears crunched, the smart car wheels spun, flinging sludge everywhere, digging itself deeper into the ground.

In his rear view mirror Gary saw Mr Buckley in his black 4x4, drive smoothly into the field, he pulled up next to the smart car. Gary stopped wheel spinning, smiled and waved. Mr Buckley got out of the jeep appropriately dressed in Hunters wellie's. Overweight Gary struggled to get out of the smart car which was now at a slight angle. He fell out awkwardly and stepped straight into deep mud. Ignoring his sinking feet, he held out his hand.

"Ah, Mr Buckley pleased to meet you."

"Hello, you must be –" Mr Buckley scrutinised his name badge. "Gay?"

Gary looked down at his badge and cussed, his R was missing. "It's Gary actually, sorry, I seem to have a problem with my R's at the moment."

Mr Buckley stared at him, weirdly. "Right, well, moving on, thanks for meeting me here, I'd like to show you the boundary lines, if that's alright with you?" He looked down at Gary's sinking shoes.

"Absolutely, no problem at all," Gary cheesy-grinned.

***

Nigel was carrying out a valuation in the neighbouring village of Willow Dean. He roamed around the manor house with Mr Clunes waddling and grunting beside him. Cobwebs swung from the ornate – if a little yellowing – chandeliers. The place was dark and smelled musty like something out of a Charles Dickens novel, cluttered with old-fashioned furniture, and the occasional torn velvet chaise longue. In need of modernisation; understatement of the century. Nigel felt like he was stuck in a time warp. As for Mr Clunes; a disgusting specimen of village royalty, his protruding pot belly bursting through the button holes of his tea-stained white shirt. His braces welded to a hula-hoop-sized waistband on corduroys smothered in egg stains from the fried breakfast he proudly told Nigel he had every single morning. Every now and then Mrs Clunes appeared. Her grey joggers and white T-shirt covered in mud and bits of leaf and just to top it off, she was wearing a bee keeper's hat. She spoke quickly, asking questions but not giving Nigel time to answer before scurrying off as quickly as she came. The viewing came to a close and they ended up where they started, in the dining room.

"What do you think?" asked Mr Clunes in his gritty plum accent.

"It was Colonel Mustard with the candlestick." Nigel guffawed.

"What are you talking about, boy?" Mr Clunes grumbled.

Nigel stood up straight, with his arms folded across his chest, and adopted his best salesman act. "This place is full of character."

Mrs Clunes reappeared, carrying a tray with a pot of tea, a biscuit, and an orange, on a yellow curling paper doily. She steered Nigel to sit at the table.

"I'd love to, but –" Nigel tapped his watch.

"You've got to eat," ordered Mrs Clunes, pushing him down into a faded orange velour chair and thrusting a soggy digestive in his face.

Like an obedient dog, Nigel sat. "I see you keep bees," he said, feigning interest.

"No I don't, I tend to find this keeps the flies off ones dinner. Terribly annoying, pesky flies, don't you find?" said Mrs Clunes in her awfully upper-class tone. "How much is it? The manor house I mean? What's it worth?"

Before Nigel could answer Mr Clunes cut-in. "But, but, Susan, what are you doing woman? I'm dealing with the estate agent, you're dealing with the gar, gardener," he stammered.

"He's got to eat, everyone's got to eat, you've got to eat, don't you find?" she glared at Nigel.

Nigel took a bite out of the stale biscuit and sipped his lukewarm tea which had skin on and was brimming with tea leaves.

"Go, go, away please, Su, Susan!" Mr Clunes stuttered, waving his hand at her.

Mrs Clunes swatted her husband's hand as if it were a fly. "You go away!"

The pair of them, wrapped in their bickering, didn't notice Nigel pour his tea into a plant and stuff the digestive in his pocket. "Thanks for the tea," he said, maneuvering out of the chair, itching to escape the madhouse. "I'll get your valuation drafted and drop it round."

Mr Clunes accompanied Nigel to the door, they stepped outside onto the big sweeping drive where the gardener was unloading tools from his van. Mr Clunes waddled quickly over to him. "You there, done already are you? Excellent," he said.

"I've only been here fifteen minutes," said the surprised gardener.

"It's drizzling now so that'll be all for today, your hourly rate ten pounds isn't it? I owe you two pounds fifty then, I suppose you'll be in need of a shit – and you," he turned to Nigel, "Do you need a shit too?"

Nigel couldn't believe his ears. The man was a total nut case. "No, I'm good thanks. I've already had one today."

"Good God man, did my wife give you one?"

Nigel looked baffled as did Mr Clunes. The gardener leaned towards Nigel. "He means a chit, its old school for invoice mate," he whispered.

Just when Nigel thought things couldn't get any more ridiculous Mrs Clunes came running towards them, waving a broom in the air at Mr Clunes.

"Su, Susan what are you doing woman?" shouted Mr Clunes, raising an arm in self- defence.

"I'm dealing with the gardener, you're dealing with the estate agent, remember?"

"I know, but it's starting to rain now Susan, and the grass, it's spun-spun."

"Spun, spun?" quizzed Mrs Clunes.

"Spongey."

"It's fine, sort of dry, dry rain, anyway, I've booked him for two hours, stop interfering."

Nigel stared at the gardener in disbelief. He laughed and signalled the cuckoo-sign.

***

This weather wouldn't do Gary's tickly cough any good. He was drenched, having foolishly left his coat in the car and his shoes were caked in thick mud. Mr Buckley on the other hand; dry as a bone, with his wax coat and umbrella, as they traipsed across the field in the pouring rain. They walked up to the house discussing the boundary. Mr Buckley removed his Hunters wellies and opened the door. He grimaced at the state of Gary's feet and mud splattered trouser legs. Smug Gary pulled out some bright orange plastic elasticated shoe protectors, squidged them over his muddy shoes and smiled.

"Code of ethics number three. Always come prepared."

CHAPTER TWO

FOXTROT OSCAR

Gary was out, Nigel was out and Rodney was out. Meaning: Lisa could indulge in a bit of *Fifty Shades* and let eager-to-impress 'posh' in her flash designer suit yak to all the customers. Downside: she had to put up with that irritating accent, worse than listening to fingernails scraping down a blackboard.

"You ought to see a doctor for that you know, love." A male builder-type customer laughed as he was going out the door.

Lucy looked bewildered. "I don't get it?"

Lisa buried her face in her book to hide her tittering, she hadn't dared speak for fear of laughing out loud.

She'd noticed it, when Lucy took her *Armani* leather jacket off first thing but chose not to tell her. Lisa had been waiting for this, the highlight of the day. She bit her bottom lip and tapped her 'Lisa' badge. Lucy glanced down at hers and glowed red. "Oh my god!" The 'R' had fallen off, it read; *Lucy anus.* "You bloody knew Lisa, didn't you?"

The door ding-a-ling broke the moment. A female customer walked in and made a beeline for Lisa's desk - always Lisa's desk, typical. "You want to see her, Miss Marple over there." Lisa waggled her finger lazily at Lucy.

"I want to see Richard Hardman, actually," announced the woman.

Lisa, without looking up, pointed to the door. "You want Brangwin & Ball across the road."

"What are you talking about? It says Hardman on your sign."

Lisa let out a sigh of boredom and bothered to lift her head. A smart, attractive, brunette, young mid-forties (because of the Botox) she guesstimated, was loitering in front of her desk, looking *exactly* like the picture in *Horse and Hound* that Nigel had shown her. She'd only been talking to *the* Mrs Buckley. Feeling like the biggest plum, Lisa tried desperately to overcompensate. "Of course, ha-ha, you're so right, Gary Hardman works here and Richard works over there." She pointed out of the window. "Take a seat I can call Gary, I mean, Richard, whatever Trevor, same thing really."

Mrs Buckley had an expression on her face similar to that of a dead cod. She looked Lisa up and down, huffed and flounced out of the door.

Lisa shook her head. "Honestly, people from Burkes End, such a bad attitude."

Lucy cut her a look. Lisa slammed her book shut and stormed out of the back door.

***

The cat that got the cream. Lady-killer Richard, placed two cups of coffee on his desk and dragged his chair around next to Mrs Buckley's. He opened his mouth to speak just as the phones blasted. "Daniel!" Richard shrieked. He was supposed to mute calls, the idiot. If hadn't have been for that interruption, Mrs Buckley wouldn't have slid her chair away, like that.

"Good afternoon the Brangwin and Ball Partnership how can I help?" Dan answered. "No sorry we don't do breakfast – we don't do beds either – no problem at all madam."

Richard frowned. "I'm getting sick of this."

"It's the fourth one today," Dan sighed.

"It's since they revamped the website and abbreviated us to B&B. I'll speak to HO, which reminds me, that important letter for head office, can you post it for me please?"

"What letter?"

"You know what letter *Dandini*."

Mrs Buckley was getting impatient. "If it's a bad time I can come back..."

"Oh that letter!" Dan grabbed an empty envelope out of his desk and made himself disappear.

***

Lisa waited around the back of the shops by the wheelie bins tapping her foot impatiently, she couldn't wait to get it off her chest. As soon as Dan appeared, she launched into one of her mega-rants. "She's driving me nuts. Miss goody two shoes. You should have seen the evils she gave me, she actually believes she's from Burkes End, she's from Aber-something-wrist-whatever, some village in Wales, the silly cow – shagger."

Ever the gentleman, Dan calmly handed her his lit cigarette and listened. In between moans Lisa chain-smoked the life out of it, before handing it back. He took one last long pull, blew a string of smoke rings, flicked the cigarette away and set his phone alarm. "We've got one minute before my cock goes off."

And so commenced the sixty second snogging session.

***

Body language; positive, toothy smiles, eye contact, huge pupils, and she kept flicking her hair back in a flirty way. Richard leaned in a little closer just as unwanted genie Dandini poofed into existence and killed the moment. Mrs Buckley stood up breaking Richard out of his love-trance.

"Thanks for coming in today Mrs Buckley – or may I call you Elizabeth?"

"No you may not, you can call me Liz, like everyone else," she gave him a curt smile. "Only my mum calls me that, when she's angry."

She held out her hand, Richard grabbed it and shook it vigorously. "Liz, it's been a pleasure, this must be such a difficult time for you." He stopped mid-flow and removed a hair from her shoulder. "We're having a B&B get together Friday night."

"We are?" Dan looked surprised.

"You'd forget your head if it wasn't screwed on." Richard gave Dan a woeful look, before averting his attention back to Liz. "Existing and potential clients welcome, if you fancy joining us for a drink, professionally speaking of course," he asked, still shaking her hand.

"I'm not going out for a drink."

"Or some peanuts?"

"No! I mean no thanks, no peanuts," she said, wrenching her hand from his grasp.

***

Gary was wandering around with his new computerized device, measuring the bedrooms. One more room to go, judging by the lavish playthings everywhere – the nursery. His tummy was rumbling and his mouth as dry as a birdcage. He'd been there forty-five minutes and not one offer of a cuppa, let alone a biscuit.

Gary tripped over a toy car crushing it in the process. He kicked it under the cot and held his fancy device against the wall. Nothing happened. He shook it and shook it – nothing. Across the room he noticed a baby monitor, maybe it was interfering with the signal. He walked over and hit the big red button. A female voice crackled through the speaker:

"What's that ghastly orange invalid vehicle doing in the bottom field?"

"That Hardman estate agents here, I asked him to meet me by the entrance but he drove onto the field for some daft reason. I doubt he'll be driving it away it's well and truly stuck in the mud."

Gary held his breath and continued eavesdropping.

"He'd better move it, or I'll get the salvage people to collect it. It's an eyesore, it's going to frighten my horses. Let's hope he's a better estate agent than he is a driver."

"He's a bit of a buffoon, but I did warm to him eventually, they're a couple of guys started up on their own. If

they don't sell they don't get paid, apparently." Mr Buckley chuckled.

"I saw the other one, Richard Hardman, they're brothers, must be rivals – peculiar."

"Well, if you can get us a better deal, be my guest, you can buy yourself another four horses with the change."

Broad-shouldered Gary could handle insults, but the thought of his brother getting the deal – the stress was too much, he couldn't hold his tickly cough in any longer, it just came out. Mr Buckley's voice crackled through the monitor.

"What was that noise?"

Gary, panicking to find the off button, pressed buttons left right and centre, nothing worked. He shook the monitor aggressively and held it up to his ear.

"I THINK I'D PREFER A SINGLES HOLIDAY ACTUALLY," Mrs Buckley boomed straight into his ear canal. Gary stumbled backwards and dropped the monitor.

"I'm off to work on the Bexley account, unless you want to talk?" He heard Mr Buckley say.

"There's nothing to talk about," came the terse female response, followed by a door slam.

***

Richard drummed his fingers on the desk, irritated. Before his phone had a chance to ring he had snatched up the receiver. "Before you say it, no – N. O."

"Richard?"

"Liz!" he almost choked, cursing under his breath at Dan like it was his fault. "What a lovely surprise."

"About those peanuts…"

***

Gary was waiting on the corner of Love Lane, in the rain. A familiar black BMW came flying round the corner and pulled up next to him. He climbed into the passenger seat and yanked the door shut aggressively. Nigel gave him the; *I-told-you-so* nod, and wheel spun off.

"Not such a *smart* car after all, is it Gary."

After a silent ride back to the office Gary strolled in the door with Nigel. Lucy was busy printing property brochures, whereas Lisa – was busy painting her nails. Gary elbowed Nigel and gave him the; *I-told-you-so* nod, it was his *smart* idea to give rubbish Lisa a third chance.

"Had any pressing emails lately, Lisa?" Gary enquired, adopting a sarcastic tone.

"Yes." Lisa blew her nails. "Don't see why you couldn't have just asked."

"Is that professional?" Gary raised his eyebrows. "You haven't done it, have you?"

"I have rung BPFS for your information, they can pick it up Friday."

"Friday!" Gary gasped.

"I did try!" Lisa whinged.

"Try, my eye. Get them on the phone, and transfer it to me. I'll show you how it's done."

Lisa tutted but did as she was told. Gary hit the loudspeaker button so everyone could hear.

"Friday's not acceptable, I need my car today, put me on to the manager," he moaned, loudly.

"I am the manager sir," said the patronising male voice out of the loudspeaker.

"I see, you own the whole of BPFS do you?" asked Gary, with a hint of sarcasm, fiddling with his cufflinks, a habit he'd taken up since he'd lost the stress ball Nigel bought him.

"No sir, I manage it. If you want to speak to the owner you'll have to send an email to Davesmith@BPFS.com."

"Oh I will, trust me," Gary moaned. "So that's Dave Smith at Papa Bravo Foxtrot Sierra."

"No, it's Bravo Papa."

"That's what I said."

"No you didn't, you said Papa Bravo."

"Whatever – B for Bravo, P for Papa, S for Sierra."

"Yes – I mean no! It's Bravo, Papa, *then* it's Foxtrot, Sierra, you're confusing me now!"

Gary huffed. "It's a terrible line, so, it's B for –."

"Bonkers," said the agitated manager.

Gary tutted. "Finally we're getting somewhere, so it's B then P."

"Yep! P for prat, F for fool and S for stupid."

Lisa and Nigel sniggered. Embarrassed Gary, hit the end call button. "Stupid phone, might as well be a paper cup and a ball of string."

"Should have told him to Foxtrot Oscar, Gaz," guffawed Nigel.

"I'm going home," Gary sulked.

"Need a lift?" asked Rodney, half-smiling, half-dumbfounded.

***

Lisa meandered into the office, hoping nobody would mention her multi-coloured bobble hat with the ear flaps hanging down, or the minor detail she was half a day late. They were lucky she even bothered, considering it was Friday.

"*Where did you get that hat, where did you get that hat?*" Nigel sang.

"Oh Nigel, you're so funny," Lucy

laughed.

Lisa cut her a look. "I've got an ear infection, alright? Stop laughing at my hat."

"We're not!" Nigel bit his lip.

"Whatever, do I look as thick as I am?" snapped Lisa.

Lucy sniggered, and Nigel let rip his booming raucous laugh, what was so funny? Idiots.

"I think it's rather fetching," half-smiled Rodney.

"Thanks od," Lisa nodded at his name badge whilst rubbing her sore ear with the flap.

Rodney looked down and noticed his R was missing too. "Oh dear, no wonder the customers looked at me strangely, they think I'm odd."

To be fair he did look a bit like a carrot – not that she would ever tell him that to his face. Well, not in so many words. "That's because you are odd, you're an odd Rod root-vegetable," Lisa smiled affectionately.

"Root- Vujasovic, actually," Rodney corrected her.

"It's easier to say root-vegetable though, innit." Nigel dirty-laughed.

Lisa's attention was thwarted. Her eyes widened the sight of a silver blimp hovering in the sky. "What on earth is that flying blob?"

"Is it a bird, is it a plane – is it Gary." Nigel belly-laughed.

"No, he's gone to get lunch, he's treating us all to pizza because it's Friday," Rodney replied.

Lisa burst into a snort. Rodney; so funny, without having to try, unlike Nigel.

"I hope there's no meat on it. I don't like meat," Lucy grimaced.

"I asked for a vegetable one," added Rodney.

"Did you ask for a root vegetable one?" Lisa smirked.

Nigel dirty laughed. "Very good Lisa."

"I love vegetables, especially baked beans," grinned Lucy.

Nigel stared at her in disbelief. "You do know a baked bean's not a vegetable, well, not in England, anyhow."

"Yes it is – isn't it?" quizzed Lucy, turning pink.

"What makes you think a baked bean is a vegetable?" Lisa probed.

"I don't know, broad bean, runner bean."

"A baked beans not a bean, it's a pulse, Lucy," Rodney informed her.

"Really?" replied Lucy, puzzled. "I thought a pulse was a thing in your wrist?"

"All I'm worried about is there being any left by the time he gets back." Nigel mimed the cross of Jesus on his body and kissed his gold crucifix.

Lucy looked at him inquisitively. Lisa explained on Nigel's behalf.

"Gary's got an eating disorder. He got caught stealing biscuits from a client, every time he did a viewing he took one. The client got wise to it, set up cameras and everything, they caught him hands down. She was so annoyed she went to Brangwin in the end."

"Ethical code number four, do not gossip about each other, behind each other's backs," Nigel raised his eyebrows. "He was worse with cheese, do you remember, Lis?"

Lisa sniggered. "He kept doing those awful cheese gasps."

"What's a cheese gasp?" quizzed Lucy.

"He gets indigestion and makes this horrible sound – *uuurgh*..." said Lisa, clutching her chest, and doing a mean impersonation of Gary.

"Ah, poor Gary, love him," replied Lucy, full of sympathy.

"It only happens if he eats too fast, best to make light of it," quipped Nigel. "Anyways, enough silly stuff, there's work to be done. Lucy, could you do a special errand for me?"

***

Richard was making coffee out the back, through the open doorway he noticed H&C's latest bit of stuff walk in. She perched herself in front of Dan's desk. Richard eyed her up and down and sucked his teeth. Not a bad looker and she had a decent set of child bearing hips. Torn between two lovers; the one who could bear his spawn, or the minted divorcee-to-be. Family life versus a shallow existence of pretentious non-stop cocktail parties. Eeny-meeny-miny-moe – the one with the hips or the one with the dough.

"Hi I'm Lucy, the new girl from H&C, pleased to meet you." Richard overheard.

Dan stood up and shook her hand. "Daniel. Nice to meet you."

Richard, still spying from the kitchen, ogled her legs as she bent down, picked up a packet of Marlboro and handed them to Dan. He grabbed them and shoved them in his desk drawer.

"You're allowed to smoke here then? I had to pretend I didn't when I went for my interview."

Dan swiftly changed the subject. "So, you're the one from Aber – Aber –."

"Never mind." Lucy sighed.

Richard emerged from the kitchen, lint rolling the arms of his navy suit. "Aber-never-mind? Sounds like something out of Peter Pan." He took the cigarette packet out of Dan's drawer, crushed it with his hand and dropped it into the waste paper basket. "What brings you over here then? Apart from the need to share your debauched love of smoking?"

Lucy blushed. "Can I use the photocopier please?"

"Yes you can," answered Dan. "No you can't," answered Richard simultaneously.

Dan shrugged his shoulders, Lucy turned to Richard, bewildered.

"But I only need –"

"Nope." Richard shook his head firmly.

"Two copies."

"No way." Richard folded his arms across his chest.

"Can I just have one then?"

"Listen, outside work if Gary wanted a copy of something, no problem at all, he's my brother, I'd do anything for him, I love him to bits, but when it comes to work –"

"They ended up having a massive fight over the copier," Dan piped up. "Caused a family feud didn't it Rich?"

Richard responded with an evil glare. Dan cleared his throat and buried his head in his work.

"That's why those two idiots sent you over here." Richard nodded toward the window.

E.A

Lucy spun around to see Nigel and Lisa grinning and waving at them through the big glass front of H&C...

***

Gary pulled up on the double yellows outside the newly opened Chico Pizza and jumped out of the car. Grown men dressed up as Spiderman wearing BOGOF boards paraded up and down. He walked up to the door of Chico Pizza then saw a traffic warden about ten metres away glaring at him. It was like a scene from; *Gunfight at the O.K Corral.* Gary's hand poised over the door handle – the warden's hand hovered over his ticket machine. Gary dared to step inside – the warden dared to pull out a ticket.

"Give me a break, I just want to get my lunch!" Gary shouted.

"Give me a break, I just want to give you a ticket!" The warden shouted back.

Gary drove slowly through level one's sea of disabled spaces, every single one; empty. Level two; no spaces. Level three; yep, you guessed it. Level four; Sainsbury's only. Level five; cinema, still no spaces. Level six; the Holy Grail, one solitary space, so narrow Gary barely managed to squeeze himself out of the car. He looked down and saw the 'B' pedal sticker stuck to the bottom of his shoe. Whatever.

Gary perched himself in front of the ticket machine, reading the instructions, scratching his head; so overcomplicated. He took his glasses out of his pocket and dropped them in a conveniently placed puddle. He bent down, picked them up and put them back on. Squinting through droplets of water he followed the instructions and typed in his registration number, the machine beeped and displayed the message; *cash only.* Typical. Gary tutted and walked over to the lift. He pushed the buttons but nothing happened, huffing and puffing he hurried down five flights of stairs. Ah-hah, there was a cashpoint-God – on the bottom floor. Gary took out a tenner and headed back to the lift. He pushed the buttons to no avail. Taking a deep breath, he braced himself and plodded back up the stairs. He examined the ticket machine, searching for where to put the money then he saw it, in tiny letters; *coins only.* Knackered and starving, frustrated Gary punched the machine and trudged back down the stairs. He was about to go into the newsagents to get change but – Chico Pizza was only three shops away.

The pizza man handed the two large pizza boxes to flustered, sweaty, ungrateful Gary. He made his way back to the car park. The lift door was open. Result!

The traffic warden was waving from a distance when he got back to the car. Gary snatched the ticket off the windscreen, drove past the traffic warden and flipped him the finger.

The smell of pizza wafted from the passenger seat. *"Go on, one slice won't hurt,"* urged his mind. "Shut up!" Gary shouted out loud. *"It smells so nice, so cheesy,"* urged his mind. Gary opened the sunroof for some air, hoping to disperse the smell of temptation. *"You've earned it. Think of all the calories you burnt running up and down those stairs."*

Gary tore open the box and grabbed a slice, he pulled and pulled, but the cheese kept stretching until he was holding it right out of the smart car sunroof. The sound of a loud beep startled him. Gary looked up to see a speeding van careering straight towards him.

CHAPTER THREE

INTELLIGENT PROSPECTING

Gary scraped stringy cheese off the steering wheel and his pink shirt. He grabbed the mangled pizza slice out of the footwell, chucked it in the food waste and went inside the house. As usual, his darling wife Lindsay was playing Candy Crush on her iPad.

"Hello darling." Gary kissed her on the head.

"Hello darling." Lindsay kissed the air. "Coffee?"

"Yes please, I'm a bit shaken, I narrowly avoided a head-on collision and almost hit a lamppost," confessed Gary, running up the stairs and disappearing into the bathroom.

"I'm on it, darling!" Lindsay called out.

"I've got about one minute!" Gary hollered, frantically scrubbing the cheese stain off his shirt. Nigel and Lisa would never let him live it down if he went into the office like that. He rushed downstairs into the kitchen. Lindsay, as per, remained glued to her iPad. He filled two cups from the coffee machine and put them on the table.

"Oh sweetie thanks," she smiled without looking up.

"Listen Linz, if we clinch this Buckley mansion it'll be the making of us, we can branch out, get more staff, and if we get the Clunes manor house, it'll be the icing on the cake, we can buy a bigger house."

"Mm-Hmm."

"And if we don't, our house will be repossessed, and we'll be homeless."

"U-huh."

"Yes, I thought that might concern you." Gary guzzled his coffee. "Got to run," he bent down and kissed her on the cheek.

"Bye darling." She kissed the air. "By the way, you've got a 'B' sticker stuck to the bottom of your shoe."

Gary strolled into the office and plonked the pizza boxes onto his desk. "It's Chico time!"

"It's about time!" exclaimed Nigel.

"I couldn't get a space."

"You what? You can park them things sideways, failing that, carry it around under your arm." Nigel guffawed. "What's that wet patch on your shirt?"

"Don't even go there, Nige."

"What flavour are they Gary?" Lucy asked.

"To be honest, I can't remember." He opened the first box. "Double pepperoni." He opened the second box. "Quadruple cheese."

"Why is there only eleven slices?" grilled Lisa.

Nigel and Lisa cut each other a suspicious look, it was obvious they were thinking; Gary had moved it around to disguise the missing slice. Again.

"That's how it came," Gary snapped, giving them both evils.

"Quadruple? Gosh, that's a lot," quipped Lucy.

"I'd stick to pepperoni if I were you, lots of meat is better than lots of cheese." Lisa winked.

"Oh my God, what do you mean meat?"

"Lucy, what do you think pepperoni is?" Lisa threw her arms in the air. "A vegetable?"

"Kind of, I thought it was peppers mixed with macaroni."

"Looks like you're going to get mad cheese disease then." Lisa put a hand to her chest and demonstrated a cheese gasp. Nigel fell about, Rodney half-smiled, Lucy stifled a chuckle.

"Very amusing," Gary retorted.

"Come on, Gazza, we're only having a laugh," Nigel chuckled.

"You wouldn't laugh if I joked that your mum had dementia."

That wiped the smile off Nigel's face. "No I wouldn't Gary, because she has got dementia."

"Come on everybody, let's stop bickering and enjoy," half-smiled Rodney.

"Rodney's right, it looks lush!" Lucy beamed.

***

Lisa sat on the paper recycle bin rubbing her bad ear with her bobble-hat flap. Someone approached from behind and startled her, she screamed and lashed out, knocking the intruder into a wheelie bin. Tea bags, banana skins and all sorts tumbled out on top of him.

"Shit! Sorry babe," Lisa giggled as she helped Dan up, together they put the rubbish back. "I'm really jumpy, it's my ear. I need some loving." She puckered her lips expectantly.

"Babe, I can't, I just needed to tell you something."

"No cock time?" she pouted.

Dan grinned. "That was wicked what you did earlier, sending Lucy over."

"Aw, I felt sorry for her – a bit. It was Nigel's idea, did Richard go ballistic?"

"No he didn't, he's in a good mood because he's got a date tonight, guess who he's pulled?"

Lisa hiccoughed. "Pardon me, bloody cheese gasps." She clutched her chest. "A mussel?"

"He'd be better off if he did I tell you."

"Who is it?"

"I'll give you a ten guesses, you'll never get it."

"The *horse and hound* hag."

"What is it with you? How do you always know things?"

"Very funny, who is it really?"

"Seriously! It *is* the Buckley woman."

"No way! Dirty little bitch."

"It's a corporate do essentially, so I'll be there too, it's about mingling with the community, intelligent prospecting Rich called it, see if you can get Gary to do the same babe, we can have a right laugh."

Lisa's attempt to sneak in the back door failed. Miss Marple was in the kitchen, faffing around with the tombola machine. She pulled out two screwed up pieces of paper.

"Hi Lisa, where have you been? You've got a pen in your pony tail by the way."

"Get a bit of fresh air, gets a bit stuffy in here, I am aware, it's so no one can steal it, thanks."

Lucy unravelled the pieces of paper and read the names aloud. "Lucy and Rodney are the two people working this weekend."

"Did you say Lisa?" asked Lisa, surprised.

"Did I say Lisa?" Lucy blushed. "I meant Lucy, as in me."

"Oh good – for you I mean, to get to grips with everything." Lisa pushed past her into the office. "Gary, I've had an idea." Gary was head down, submerged in paperwork. "I think we should have an office get together in the Adam and Eve tonight."

Gary lifted his head and sighed. "And why would I want to do that Lisa, pray tell?"

"To mingle with the community, it's what your brothers doing, intelligent prospecting he called it, well, that's what I heard anyway."

Lucy rushed into the office. "Lisa, that's a fab idea! I'm well up for it!"

"Hands up, for yes." Lisa raised her arm.

Lucy and Nigel threw their arms into the air, as did Rodney, albeit a little slower.

"Hmm." Gary puckered his brow. "Can't have him getting one up on us can we, Adam and Eve it is, 7.30pm sharp."

"Cool." Lisa grinned. "By the way Lucy, your shirt's ripping."

Lucy smiled. "Aw thanks, I got it in Burkes End market, it was only a fiver."

"No Lucy, it's ripping, under the arm, look."

Lucy lifted her arm and gasped. "Oh my God! I thought you meant *ripping* was English for cool or something, like we say lush in Welsh for lovely."

Lisa burst out laughing. Lucy did too.

"I'm so looking forward to the pub tonight," Lucy gleamed, her eyes full of excitement.

"Me too," agreed Lisa, and strangely, she meant it.

***

Gary returned from the bar with a tray full of drinks. Pinot Grigio for the girls, Guinness for Nigel, a bitter lemon for teetotal Rod and a pink gin and tonic with a slice of lime for himself.

"Remember gang, everyone's a potential customer, keep in mind the WOW code. Cheers everyone!" Gary raised his glass. Nigel, Lisa, Lucy and Rodney raised theirs.

Nigel pointed at the bar. "Look who's just walked in Gazza – Casanova, whose he pulled now? Honestly, your brother has a different bird every week."

"I best go and check," said Gary, concerned. "Don't want him getting that disease again."

"Aw, love him, you're so caring Gary," Lucy gushed.

Yes he was caring, deep down, underneath his professional persona. Gary grabbed his drink, made his way over to the bar and tapped Richard on the shoulder. "Do you come here often?"

Richard spun around. "Ugh, what do *you* want?" he moaned.

"Never answer a question with a question, Dickie damp pants," Gary mocked him.

"Do you want me to say your nickname?" Richard sneered.

"Calm down, Mr Snooty, just being polite, aren't you going to introduce me to your *friend?*"

"This is Gary," Richard let out a sigh of boredom, "my big brother."

Gary shook the lady's outstretched hand. "Pleased to meet you."

"So pleased he wants to buy you a drink," Richard smirked, "while I nip to the loo."

He disappeared leaving an awkward silence. Gary's

attempt to lighten the atmosphere.

"Sorry about him, he gets nervous on dates, he probably needs to deflate." It fell flat, she looked at him disgusted. "What can I get you to drink?" asked Gary, rapidly moving on.

"I'll have a large Moet, please." The lady smiled.

"Shall I add that to your tab, sir?" enquired the barman.

"No, put it on Brangwins." Gary smirked, gloating in the smug joy of brotherly one-upmanship.

***

Lisa craned her neck, scanning the crowd trying to spot Dan. Instead, she spotted Gary handing a glass of champagne to you-know-who. She gasped in horror.

"What's the matter Lisa?" Lucy asked.

"A man who makes mats," Nigel laughed.

"I don't get it?" Lucy looked confused.

"Me either," admitted dumbfounded Rodney.

"You said; *what's a matter,* he said *a man who makes mats* – oh forget it." Lisa rolled her eyes. "More importantly Nigel, look over there, Gary's talking to the *horse and hound* hag."

"Don't worry, I'm sure she'll work out he's a closet." Nigel laughed.

"Nigel!" Lisa was freaking out. "The woman at the bar, it's Mrs Buckley!"

Nigel chuckled. "Stop winding me up Lis, you're worse than me."

"I'm not, it's her I'm telling you, I recognise her, from when she came into the office."

"As if she'd be in this shit-hole dive."

Lucy peered over Lisa's shoulder. "Oh my God, she's right!"

Nigel turned around and almost fell off his chair. "Holy cow!" He rushed over to the rescue.

***

Gary was deep in conversation with Richard's *friend*, so much so, he chose to ignore Nigel over her shoulder trying to get his attention. The big baby could get his own bloody pint. He was busy – intelligent prospecting.

"Absolutely," agreed Gary. "To be honest, the prices are astronomical you can get twice the house for half the money up here in Waddley Bottom, only a berk would live in Burkes End."

"Is that so?" she smiled, politely.

Gary was struggling to concentrate, what with Nigel doing a silly dance and making weird gestures behind her back. He ushered Nigel to go away, too late, she turned around.

"Hello." Nigel gulped. "I was just admiring your dress it's um – rather WOW isn't it, Gary."

"This is my partner and stand-up comedian, Nigel," Gary, declared, rocking on his heels. "Nige, this is um – well anyway, we were discussing how snobby people are in Burkes End."

"Sorry I had to dash." A dishevelled Richard appeared, smoothing down his hair and tucking his shirt back in. "Didn't finish introducing you, did I? Gary, this is Liz – Liz Buckley, she's selling her house in Burkes End."

"You know, that place where all the berks live," she smiled sweetly.

Gary's jaw hit the floor, as did his pink gin and tonic.

***

Gary, Nigel and Rodney were talking shop. Lisa was drowning her sorrows about Dan's no-show, guzzling wine with Lucy and gossiping about everything under the sun. It turned out Lucy wasn't such a bad egg, in fact she was quite a funny egg.

"I love your top Lucy, it's really pretty."

"Aw thanks, it's a bit tight now that I'm two stone overweight."

"You don't look it." Lisa was surprised.

"I was eight stone until a year ago, I fancied this boy that worked in Greggs so I went there every lunch time for like six months."

"And you kept buying cakes?" Lisa suggested knowingly, as she slurped her wine.

"Exactly, and pasties, by the time I'd plucked up courage to ask him out I'd ballooned up to ten stone, then guess what he said? *Sorry love, I only go for slim girls*. I was so heartbroken, I told all my mates at uni and we boycotted the place, it shut down in the end."

"Excellent," Lisa clapped her hands together with glee. "Is that why you moved down here?"

"Not really, I'd have better prospects my mum reckoned, but it's not that, it's because she wanted to get away from the valleys, she's celebrity obsessed and wants to be a TV presenter. Anyways, enough about me, how long have you worked at H&C?"

"Two years, ever since they started the company, I used to work for Brangwin with Gary, until he got made redundant."

"Gary worked for Brangwin? What – with Richard?"

"Yeah, Gary was MD for ten years, he even got Richard the job, taught him everything, and then they went and gave Richard his job, can you imagine."

"Oh my God, are you serious? Poor Gary, love him."

"He got depressed and put on loads of weight, then his wife left him, she's such a bitch, she only went back with him because he started the company. She didn't give a shit when the bailiff went round to take all his stuff."

"Poor Gary, that's so harsh, what a nasty man taking all his stuff."

"He didn't, he loaded up the van then put it all back, that nasty man turned out to be Nigel."

"Oh my god, what, Nigel, Nigel?"

"Yep, you know that scar on his face? He's got a massive one across his chest, some gangster bloke slashed him with a chainsaw when Nigel tried to take his TV then he threatened to cut his face open and take his gold tooth."

"That's awful. I can't get over Nigel being a bailiff."

"Yeah, he got stitched up – literally, a hundred of them, poor bugger, he was a Kirby cleaner salesman before that, culture shock eh."

"I don't get it, why did Nigel give Gary his stuff back?"

"Don't tell anyone." Lisa lowered her voice. "Gary tried to hang himself, Nigel went in for the TV and had to cut him down, anyway, they started talking and it turned out Nigel was pissed off with his job so they decided to start H&C, they went to see Rod and he gave them the money to start up."

"That's awful, poor Gary, it's sort of like a love story, who's Rod?"

"You know, odd Rod over there, he was their bank manager."

"No way! Rodney was a bank manager, aw love him."

"Yeah, keep your voice down, he was, but I wouldn't trust him with my money." Lisa glanced around the guys were busy talking shop. "I don't know if I should tell you this…"

"Oh my God, I love rumours, go on, I won't say anything, pinky promise." Lucy whispered.

***

Half of Gary was concentrating on Nigel pouring his heart out about his mum, the other half was being eaten alive with paranoia over Richard's little soiree with Mrs Buckley at their cosy little corner table. He couldn't take another second of it and off he stomped to gate-crash a certain party for two.

"Sorry to intrude," he blurted. "Richard, can I have a word please?"

"No – there you go, there's a word."

"It's okay guys, I need to powder my nose, see you in a tick – Dickie," said Mrs Buckley grinning and trundling off to the ladies.

"I thought you were having an office do, where's Daniel?" Gary frowned.

"He couldn't make it, *oh-kay*?" Richard let out a groan. "Why am even I telling you this, golden rule, we don't discuss work, remember?"

"I don't want to talk about work, Rich. I'm worried, seriously, if her husband finds out."

"He won't, he's away working with some blonde bird, anyway, they're getting a divorce she can do what she likes."

"You're playing with fire, Rich."

"Get a life Gary, the only thing you're worried about is me getting the business."

"Rich, I've already seen Mr Buckley and done a valuation," Gary patronised.

"How much?"

"Three percent."

"Liar."

"I've done the deal, it's in the bag. Look, I don't give a stuff about that, it's you I'm worried about, acting like a ladies man, you've been like this ever since Kate."

"Get over Kate, I was sixteen!"

"You cried for three days solid, she damaged you, didn't she? Admit it, and that's why you sleep around, because you're desperate to find love – this one's got dogs and horses, you do realise she'll be covered in hair, it'll never work."

"It's a one night stand."

"Really? How many farts did you do when you went to the toilet?"

"One, can you please leave me to get on with my date."

"How many?"

"Alright, seven, now go away."

"I knew it, you're smitten."

***

Lucy gawped at Lisa. "Rodney? Stole money from the bank? No, I don't believe it, really?"

"He did it for those two, to start the business but he got found out, the SFO hauled him in."

"I can't believe Rodney would do that, what's the UFO thing?"

"Serious fraud office, he was interrogated and everything, when they questioned where the money was he said, *I haven't got a clue,* that's why he says it all the time, it kind of stuck, a handy tick, in case anyone asks him about it, well, that's what Dan reckons Richard reckons."

"Oh poor Rodney, did he go to prison?"

"Nah, they couldn't prove it so they had to let him off but they sacked him, that's why he works here, Gary and Nigel felt sorry for him so they gave him a job. Dan told me, you know Dan, the one who works with Richard?"

"As in your boyfriend," Lucy grinned.

"How do you know?"

"I saw his message on Facebook. I've known since my first day when you went for your *fresh air,* break."

"Please don't tell anyone," Lisa begged. "I've already had two verbal warnings, if Gary finds out he'll sack me for sure."

***

"Stop pretending you care about my welfare," Richard sneered.

Gary cracked, he couldn't keep up the pretence any longer. "Fine. Just don't try and manipulate this deal away from me Richard."

"We don't do this Gary."

Desperate, Gary held his hands together in a prayer position. "Please Rich, it's alright for you, you get a salary it's different for me and Nige, if we don't get work..."

"*We don't get paid,*" Richard mimicked. "Don't waste your bullshit sales pitch on me Gary, if I don't get work, I don't get my bonus!" he snapped.

Like an angel, seemingly out of nowhere, Nigel materialised and dragged Gary away with his hands still in the prayer position. "Come on mate, let's get you some pork scratchings."

Gary handed tipsy Lisa and Lucy a tenner and bundled them into a taxi. He clambered into the passenger seat of the smart car, Nigel squashed in, next to him. Rod reversed slowly out of the carpark, suddenly there was a crunch. Nigel leapt out of the car.

"Gazza, give us a hand mate," he shouted.

Preoccupied with checking the precious bodywork with his keyring torch, Gary suddenly noticed the whimpering old lady in a motorised wheelchair rammed into the bush. He watched Nigel struggling to heave it upright then rushed over. And there it was, a tiny scuff on the bumper.

"You scratched my car!" Gary shone the torch in her eyes.

"It wasn't her fault! Are you alright, my love?" caring Nigel asked.

"I'm fine, a little shaken. I ran out of cat food, pesky cats got to eat, all my fault, I only need it at night, my legs seize up," waffled the lady, shielding her eyes from the dazzling light.

"But you've got no lights! I hope you've got insurance for that wretched heap! People like you shouldn't be on the road, you loony bin on wheels!" Gary yelled.

"Gary shut-up!" Nigel cut-in. "Allow me to introduce you to Mrs Clunes – the lady of the manor house in Willow Dean, also our prospective client."

CHAPTER FOUR

DICKIE DAMP PANTS

"About last night, I'm so sorry Gary, there was no 'B' sticker on the pedal, I didn't know what to do," rambled Rodney, looking extra dumbfounded.

"My life," Gary mumbled under his breath.

"Did you say, my wife?" quizzed Rodney.

Why would I say that, you stupid old fool Gary wanted to say but didn't. Even though he was still bristling over last night, he didn't have the heart to be mean, not to Rod.

Lucy skipped through the door. "Bacon sarnies on a Saturday morning, lush." Her happy smile vanished when she saw Gary emerging from the kitchen. Somewhat sheepish she handed Rodney his baguette. "I didn't realise you were coming in today."

"So I gathered," frowned Gary, grabbing a tin of air freshener out of his drawer and plonking it on her desk. "I don't want this place smelling like a greasy spoon café."

"Sorry." Lucy blushed. "Gary, before you go, Mrs Buckley rang."

"Ha! Good," Gary clapped his hands, triumphantly.

He knew his brother would blow it. Dickie damp pants had fallen right into his devious three percent trap and gone in at two and a half, thinking he could undercut him. What he didn't know is, clever Gary had really quoted two percent. This day was getting better already. He rubbed his hands together like Fagin.

"Get the brochure printed Lucy, I'll hand deliver it myself."

"Um, you might be jumping the gun a bit."

"Of course, she probably wants to discuss which photo's to use, I did get some superb arty shots, she'll be spoilt for choice," Gary cut-in, with an air of smug self-righteousness.

"She didn't say about that either."

Gary tutted. "What did she say?"

"She, um, said –."

"Spit it out, child."

"When do you plan on getting rid of that heap stuck in her field?"

"Goodness me, don't tell me it's still there. They were supposed to be picking it up yesterday afternoon. Is it still there?"

"I asked her that, and she said, *unless the sun has fallen out of the sky and landed in my field, then yes.*"

An awkward silence followed as Gary's pride went out of the window.

Lucy went on. "So, I told her you'd complain to the owner of the company and sort it out."

"Oh, I will, don't you worry about that, one call from me, I can assure you heads will roll."

"Phew." Lucy wiped her brow. "That's a relief, she said her husband's arranging to have it crushed if it hasn't gone when he gets back on Monday."

"Right." Gary clicked his fingers. "Get them on the phone *now* Lucy."

"I've already tried, but they didn't answer, so I googled it, they're closed weekends."

Gary gulped nervously.

***

Richard was in seventh heaven, there wasn't the tiniest bit of fluff on his suit, and Liz was sitting opposite him. This could only mean one thing, he had the deal in the bag. The way she was ogling him with those sad puppy eyes...

"I'm going to be practically homeless, in a tiny detached four bed or something, I need to save as much money as possible – on the agent's fees – perhaps."

"How does two and a half percent sound?"

"Rubbish actually, your brother quoted two percent."

"Oh did he now – I bet he also said, *if he doesn't sell they don't get paid*, didn't he?"

"That's precisely what he said, to my husband, my ex-husband to be, that is."

"It's bullshit. I can do you a much better deal, how does one and a half percent grab you?"

"Wait a minute, that's a saving of –" She started counting on her fingers.

"Thirty thousand, five hundred and two pounds and sixty pence," Richard proudly declared.

"Really? You would do that, for me?" she fluttered her eyelashes. "Dickie..."

"I'd like to think we're, well, *good* friends," Richard winked. "Call it mate's rates, I have the power to sort that out, we could discuss it, at mine later, over some more bubbly."

"Morning guys!" Dan breezed in the door.

Bugger Dandini – the master of bad timing. Just as they were getting to the good bit. And she had called him Dickie in an endearing way. She wasn't just buttering him up, there was definitely something there he could feel it.

Liz grabbed her bag ready to leave. "Richard, tell you what, how about you come to the house Monday, my husband's away until the evening, we can go over it then?"

Say no more…

***

Gary threw his phone down and punched the dashboard, didn't matter, it was only Nigel's BMW. He was sick of hearing; *sorry there's no-one here to take your call.* Ringing them repeatedly wasn't going to change the fact BPFS weren't open until Monday. Damn it.

Gary opened the front door. The house was like a morgue. "Darling?" No answer. "Call Loo-loo," he instructed his mobile.

"What's up?" An out of breath female voice hollered through the speaker.

"Nothing's up, where are you, I thought we were going for lunch?"

"I can't, I'm at Pilates, I did say," she puffed and panted. "Then I'm having a girlfriend lunch, then we're going clothes shopping, then onto the theatre to see a show, after that we're having cocktails at

Capriccio, speak later darling." The line went dead.

Gary opened his man-bag, took out his iPad and tuned in to the office-cam he'd secretly set up that morning. Lisa and Rod were in the kitchen. Rod was scat-singing, washing up cups, Lucy was fiddling with the tombola machine trying to open it. Having nothing better to do, he grabbed the family pack of Revels that were hiding in his sock drawer, stretched himself out on the sofa and cranked up the iPad volume. The conversation was a bit muffled but he could just about decipher what they were saying.

"I looked in the diary this morning, Rodney you've been here for the last three Saturdays."

"Have I? I haven't got a clue, Lisa's in charge of that thing."

"It was me and Gary last week, you and Nigel before that, and you and Gary the week before." Lucy forced open the tombola, four pieces of screwed up paper fell out. Gary watched as she unravelled them and read the names out. "Gary, Nigel, Rodney, Lucy and – Lucy? My names in here twice! I bloody knew it, everyone's name is in here, bar Lisa. You've probably been here every Saturday since the dawn of time haven't you?"

"I've honestly got no idea."

"Rodney, I hope you don't mind me saying, but you don't seem to remember much do you?"

"No, I don't, I used to have a brilliant memory," he mused. "I used to be known as *the chimp* at university, many moons ago."

"Aw, I don't think you look like a chimp, you're more like *Ludo*, you know, in *Labyrinth*."

"Chimps have photographic memories, at least, I think that's why they called me that. I don't really remember, see? I've got a terrible memory these days."

"You poor thing, what happened to you? I mean, was it a gradual thing? Or, did something happen to make your memory go like that?"

Gary zoomed in. "I can't talk about it," said Rodney, nervously.

"You can tell me Rodney, you can trust me."

"I don't know if I should. I've never told anybody this before."

"Rodney, cross my heart and hope to die, I won't tell a soul."

"Don't do it, Rod!" Gary leapt up and bellowed at the screen, the revels fell off his lap and rolled out onto the floor. He had to stop Rod confessing, but by the time he'd got to the office Rod would already have told her, plus he would have missed the juicy bit and he was getting into it now. Ten second rule – he picked the revels up, blew off the carpet fibres and stuffed them into his mouth. He was too engrossed in the *Rodney and Lucy Show* to switch off now, the best was yet to come. Gary cranked the volume up a bit more.

"I used to work at the bank. I was the branch manager, but something bad happened and I had to leave." Rodney let out a big sigh.

"Oh wow, what a brilliant job, why did you have to leave?"

"I was in the vault one day, I had to get an important document out of the filing cabinet but the draw was jammed, so I pulled it really hard and a heavy box file fell off the top and hit me on the head."

Lucy giggled. "Sorry Rodney it's nerves, makes me laugh sometimes."

"It was a tall cabinet, hit me from a great height."

Lucy burst into hysterics. Rod looked disappointed. Gary tutted at the screen.

"Rodney, that's *so* not funny," Lucy cried, whilst laughing her head off. "Sorry, carry on, ahem." She cleared her throat in a desperate attempt to muffle the escaping giggles.

"It knocked me out cold and when I woke up I couldn't remember a thing, all those figures, all those years of training, my email addresses, everything, gone."

"Oh my God, Rod, you poor sod, that's terrible!"

Lucy wiped the tears of laughter from the corners of her eyes. "Then what happened?"

"Nothing, I didn't tell anyone, I just carried on with my job as best I could, but I made so many mistakes, and then I did something *really* bad..."

The back door opened, startling Lucy and Rod. In jogged Nigel, red and sweaty, fresh from his Saturday morning run.

"Bloody hell, Nige, I hate cliff-hangers," Gary moaned at the screen. "Just as they were getting to the juicy bit."

"Morning all, blimey what's up you two, you look like you've seen a ghost," panted Nigel.

"I was just saying, I um, wanted to talk to you Nigel –" Lucy winked at Rodney, "about the tombola."

Nigel jogged past them into the office. Gary switched to office view. Nigel was sifting through the filing cabinet. "I've got to get this valuation to poor old Mrs Clunes and make sure she's alright after Gary's antics last night. So much for the WOW code and his *everyone's a potential customer* speech. Does my head in sometimes, he's a brilliant estate agent, taught that brother of his everything he knows, outside work he's a nightmare. I mean, I like to call a spade a spade and all that, but when it comes to work we've got to cover each other, no talking about each other behind each other's backs, and no gossip. Here guys, why's he going in there?"

"Why's who going in where?" Rodney surfaced from the kitchen. Lucy followed with the tombola machine tucked under her arm, spraying air freshener around the place.

"Dickie damp pants, he never goes in on a Saturday, ah here it is." Nigel pulled out a file. "Wait a minute, have I been talking non-stop? I have haven't I? It's that bloody Speedyade, it's supposed to be an energy drink but all it does is make you rabbit, anyway babe, what were you saying, something about the tombola?"

"I um, well it's just, I mean, I hate to gossip."

Nigel snatched the tombola off her and examined it. "You broke it didn't you."

"Well yeah, kind of accidentally on purpose."

"Don't worry about it babe, I'll get Lis to get us another one, that's her job, got to get her to do something, she needs a lot of motivating that one. I've got to get out of this sweaty stuff and into me suit then I'm off to the Clunes, that's if bloody Gary hasn't messed the deal up. I only popped in to get the file and the smart car, Gary insisted, reckons it will impress them. I reckon it's because he don't want you driving it no more Rod, mind you it suits me, the sun's shining, I can open the sunroof and not have to sit with me head cocked to one side. Honestly, Gary's got no idea what it's like for me, then

I'm off to Oxbridge to see me mum, you can shut up shop at two if it's quiet. Shit, I'm rabbiting again aren't I? I feel high as a kite, I better go before my flipping jaw falls off."

Nigel grabbed a bottle of water out of the fridge and left. Maybe Gary should turn the iPad off. It wasn't such a good idea spying, he'd heard some hurtful stuff he really didn't want to hear. He was about to switch it off when Lucy muttered something...

"I can't believe how much she gets away with. I reckon she knows something, like blackmail, too many secrets around here. What's she got on them, I wonder?"

"I've got no idea," half-smiled Rodney.

Oh well, at least Nigel had thwarted posh Lucy from her probing. Gary switched it off, he'd heard more than enough for one day, plus there were no more revels.

Gary drummed his fingers on the coffee table, staring at the iPad, he caved in and switched it back on. He had to be sure the gossiping had stopped. Lucy and Rodney were at their desks, Rod was doing the crossword Lucy was reading, not much to see. Excellent, some good had come of Nigel's interruption, it had diverted the nosey welsh dog with a bone off the scent. Gary was about to switch it off when Lucy muttered something, again.

"Rodney? You were going to tell me something before Nigel came in weren't you?"

"Bloody hell!" Gary shouted at the screen. Lisa wasn't wrong calling her Miss Marple.

"Was I, I don't remember?"

"Oh, come on Rodney, try, it'll be good exercise for your memory, you did something really bad you were saying?"

"Oh, that. I don't know if I should tell you. I've never told anyone this before, nobody knows about it, apart from Gary and Nigel."

"Well they would wouldn't they, I think I know what you're going to tell me Rodney, about the bad thing that happened, was it something to do with money?"

Gary was intrigued, how the hell did she know?

"Yes it was. Lots of money, lots and lots actually," Rodney whistled through his teeth.

"How much?"

"Hundreds of millions of pounds."

"Oh my God, Rodney! What have you done with the money?"

Gary stuffed his fist into his mouth and bit his knuckles.

***

Happy, whistling, Richard bounced back in the door after seeing Liz to her car. Dan was talking on the

E.A

phone, shaking his head at him in despair.

"No sir, we're not false advertising – we're as fed up as you sir – I will pass that on – thank you sir, bye now." He put the phone down. "Seriously boss, it's getting worse the phone hasn't stopped since you walked out the door."

It rang again. Dan attempted to answer but Richard put his hand in the air. He winked at Dan, calmly smoothed the invisible creases out of his tie and picked up the phone.

"Good morning the Brangwin and Ball Partnership, how can I help – no we're full up I'm afraid madam – yes for the whole season madam, sorry about that – no problem at all – thanks for the call."

"That is genius, sheer genius." Dan was full of admiration. "I'm going to say that next time."

"This is going to be a long half-day," Richard sighed.

***

"Oh there was no money," Rodney declared. "It was on the computer. I was doing the yearly accounts and input hundreds of millions as a debit instead of a credit, almost forced the bank into liquidation, caused a big stir, the SFO got involved, they thought I was up to no good and trying to steal money."

"And were you?"

"Was I what?" quizzed Rodney, dumbfounded.

"Up to no good?"

"Good Lord no. I might be a fool but I'm not a thief. It was an accident, all I did was simply push the wrong buttons and as a result it cost me my job."

"Oh Rodney, I knew you were innocent." Lucy leapt out of her chair and gave him a big hug.

"My wife made me got to the doctors, turned out I'd suffered a brain haemorrhage from the box file injury and I didn't even know it, that's why I was malfunctioning, stupid old fool."

"You're not a stupid fool, it's not your fault, none of it. Now I understand why you hate computers so much."

"I loathe computers. The doctor instructed me to get a less stressful job so here I am."

"Aw Rodney, that's so sad."

Gary was engrossed. This really was better than *Coronation Street, Eastenders* and even *El Dorado*, he used to love that show, such a shame it was axed.

"Don't be sorry, I'm happy here, if it wasn't for Nigel and Gary I don't know where I'd be," Rodney smiled wistfully.

Gary put a hand on his heart and dabbed an invisible tear from the corner of his eye.

"So, before you started here, you were their bank

manager, were you?" Lucy went on.

"Yes, I authorised their start-up loan, in fact it was the H&C box file that hit me on the head that day. I told Gary and Nigel what happened and they felt so bad they gave me a job. I don't know anyone else that would put up with my terrible memory."

"Oh Rodney," Lucy cocked her head to one side. "I think you're a hero, you remind of that bloke in that film," she pondered, dreamily.

"Buck Rogers?"

"No, not him, but you're on the right track, he's really good looking."

"Something to do with a bank job?" asked Rodney.

"Ocean's eleven!" Gary shrieked. "Me being George Clooney, obviously."

"I've got it! Tom Hanks!" squealed Lucy.

Rodney beamed.

"Forrest Gump, that's the one."

Rodney's smile faded. "More appropriate I suppose," he whistled through his teeth. "My memory is awful ask me a question? Go on, ask me how many pens I've got in my pen pot."

"How many pens have you got in your pen pot?"

"I've got no idea – see?"

Lucy giggled. "Oh Rodney, that's a hard question, nobody would know the answer to that."

"Ask me another one then, ask me what year I was born."

"What year were you born?"

"I've got no idea – see? How ludicrous it is?"

"Well, Rodney Root-thingy-ma-jig, I think you're brilliant, you're a lovely man and I won't tell a soul. I pinky promise you that. Fancy a cup of tea?"

"I'll make it, you like early grey don't you?"

"See, you do remember, the important things," encouraged Lucy.

"Oh no he doesn't!" Gary boomed as Rodney made his way into the kitchen. "She's behind you!" he yelled, slapping his knee repeatedly.

Rodney stopped in his tracks, directly underneath the camera. "I remember something else, too. A couple of weeks ago, I stood in for Nigel and did a viewing for a wealthy gentleman in Burkes End, I haven't told Gary this but – his wife Lindsay was there."

Gary stopped laughing. "Collecting things for charity, probably." He wiped a sweaty hand on his leg, feeling strangely anxious.

Rodney looked up, straight into the camera. "I went in to measure the bedroom and..."

Gary hit the off button. He'd heard enough tittle tattle for one day. Honestly, they weren't paid to sit and gossip. It was a bad idea getting an office cam, a super-quadruple *bad* idea. He only got one because they were cheap on eBay, it was probably from China. He flipped it over, and saw the sticker on the back; *made in Taiwan*. There you go, absolute piece of rubbish, malfunctioning and not recording conversations properly. Gary elbowed the iPad off the coffee table. It landed with a thud on the floor.

CHAPTER FIVE

THE FREAK SHOW

Nigel was bang on time, probably because his head was acting like a bloody sundial poking out of the smart car sunroof. Eccentric nut-bag Mrs Clunes came rushing over to greet him in her bee keeper's hat. Nigel crossed his heart, kissed his gold crucifix and got out of the car.

"Hello Mrs Clunes, how are you? Are you okay?"

"I'm fine, honestly, right as rain, no broken bones, see?" She jiggled her arms then wiggled her legs like a demented chicken.

"I'm very pleased to hear that."

"Your chubby partner was right, it was my fault. I taped some candles to the front but they blew out before I got to the end of the drive, handy things candles but no good if it's windy."

"I'm so sorry Mrs Clunes, I would hate for us to, I mean, for you to –"

"Don't worry, I'm not going to go elsewhere, can't be doing with people, meeting people, strangers, pesky nuisance."

"In that case, here you go." Nigel smiled broadly and handed her the valuation file.

"Drat, one need's one's glasses, can't see a pesky thing without them, here." She handed the file back. "Take this to Mr C, over there by the hedge, see?" She pointed. "You can't miss him, he's wearing a sweaty vest covered in tea stains."

Nigel walked tentatively over to Mr Clunes; wearing headphones and pruning the hedge with a chainsaw. His attempt to not startle him backfired, Mr Clunes stumbled back waving the chainsaw dangerously near Nigel's face before clumsily dropping it, and narrowly missing his own foot. The chainsaw spiralled out of control, taking chunks of hedgerow with it. Nigel wrestled it and managed to hit the off switch before it could do any further damage. Mr Clunes removed his headphones, he was sweating profusely, swaying and rubbing his arm.

"It's alright Sir, I've got it. I'm quite used to people

waving chainsaws about in my face."

Mr Clunes looked pale and could hardly string a sentence together. "I, I, I, we, we, we," he stammered.

"Are you alright, Mr Clunes?" asked Nigel, concerned.

Mrs Clunes came rushing over. "It's a terrible infliction he has, gets stuck sometimes, he got stuck for *two* hours one time, I had to hit him over the head with a cucumber. Cedric? What's going on? Don't make me hit you, you look terrible. Come on deep breaths, like this," she demonstrated, taking big deep breaths in then out.

Nigel stood watching the freak show unfold. Overgrown jelly baby, Mr Clunes copied his wife and his breathing slowly returned to normal.

"I'm fine Susan, s, s, stop f, f, fussing," he stuttered, pushing her away.

"Charming man isn't he?" Mrs Clunes threw her arms in the air. "Ungrateful, un-charming, get on with it then." She grabbed the file off Nigel and put her glasses on. "Golly. 1.5 million? I thought it would be at least 1.8. I suppose it's the house, bit old, could do with a tickle, haven't seen the feather duster, have you Ced? I bet you've been using it to do that thing again, haven't you?"

"1.5 is fine. Stop interfering Su, Susan," Mr Clunes coughed and spluttered. "I'm dealing with the estate agent."

"And I was dealing with the gardener until you took over, not a good idea either by the look of you, I told you not to get rid of the gardener."

Nigel couldn't take it a moment longer. "Guys, I've got to go, thrash it out amongst yourselves. I'll give you a call in a day or so, we can discuss whether you want to redecorate, push the price up."

"Good god man, redecorate, bit unnecessary isn't it?" Mr Clunes was visibly shocked.

"He means housework, don't you?" Mrs Clunes cut in. "Simple, bit of dusting, little hoovering, type thing."

"As I said, let's go through it Monday, I've got another client to see so I really must go."

"Gosh, on a Saturday as well, no time for anything, I hope you make time to eat? Got to eat, here, take this." Mrs Clunes held out an orange.

"Su, Susan! Stop interfering."

"He's got to eat, and we're out of biscuits, incredibly handy food, oranges I mean, don't you find?" She stared at Nigel curiously.

"Leave the man alone Susan, of course he doesn't want a bloody orange."

"It's not a blood orange, it's a Jaffa, juicy and sweet, he can take it then, here, take it with you." She thrust a shrivelled orange into Nigel's hand. He mumbled goodbye and starting backed away.

As soon as Nigel was safely far away enough, he turned around, legged it back to the car, jumped in and sped off. "*Got to eat, got to eat,*" he impersonated.

First a soggy biscuit now a rock hard orange, bloody lunatics. Nigel launched the orange out of the sunroof. It flew through the air like a cricket ball and landed the other side of the hedge. With a bit luck it might hit Mr Clunes on the head and cure his terrible infliction.

***

The sun was shining. The birds were singing. The queue for Café Olé was out the poxy door. All because of a silver blimp hovering in the sky advertising free coffee. Lisa's patience was stretched to the max. Thankfully, she was next in line to be served.

"I'll have a Grande super skinny sugar free caramel cappuccino extra light chocolate sprinkles wet no froth – oh and extra hot, please," demanded the snobby cow in front.

Lisa sighed loudly. "Get your money's worth," she muttered under her breath.

The lady spun round. Shoot! It was only the bloody *Horse and Hound* hag.

"Do you have a problem with that?" she glared at Lisa.

"Not at all," Lisa back-peddled, "wait until you hear mine."

"What can I get you?" asked the barista.

"Same as her, without the chocolate sprinkles but with extra froth and can you upgrade mine to the Arabica beans please? Oh, and a babyccino, for him." She glanced down at her three-year-old little boy, holding onto her leg with one hand and pointing a plastic gun at what's-her-face with the other.

Unperturbed by being held at gunpoint the *Horse and Hound* woman softened when she saw Joe. "Aren't you a cutie pie," she gushed, ruffling his blonde hair before walking off.

"Mummy, I'm going to play with the Lego." Joe darted off to the kid's area which just so happened to be right next to the psycho bitch from hell's table, she'd bagged the last one, jammy bitch. Lisa followed Joe, her eyes searching aimlessly for somewhere to sit.

"Sit here if you want," offered the *Horse and Hound* hag.

Wow, she was being nice? Must be national hag-holiday – day. Annoyingly, Lisa had no choice so she sat. "Thanks."

"What a beautiful boy you have, you're very lucky." Mrs Buckley's face smiled, but there was a sadness in her eyes. Lisa felt uncomfortable, she didn't know how to respond. Luckily she didn't have to, Mrs Buckley spoke. "Apologies, if I smell of tack," she grimaced.

"Uh-uh," Lisa shook her head and sipped her coffee. "I love horses."

"Me too." The woman smiled and held out her hand. "I'm Liz."

Lisa shook her hand. "Lisa, or as Gary prefers to call me, poor Lisa."

"Why?"

"Because I'm from Marshfield."

"Rude. I'm from Marshfield and look at me, I've nothing to be ashamed of."

"No way!"

How random. From that moment on they clicked. Lisa chatted to the *Horse and Hound* woman as if they were best friends – who knew. They were engrossed in conversation about growing up in the slums of Marshfield, seamlessly onto horses, which somehow led to love and loss. Lisa found herself pouring her heart out.

"He was the love of my life, we'd been together for two months when he died."

Liz's hand flew to her mouth. Tears welled up in her eyes. "I'm so sorry, that's terrible."

"I know it doesn't sound long but we really bonded in that time." Lisa swallowed hard.

"The poor horse." Liz dabbed her eyes with her cuff. "Not like it's just a dog or anything."

"Crying in a coffee shop, what are we like," snivelled Lisa, fighting the waterworks, she wasn't one to cry easily but horses – different matter.

"This will cheer you up." Liz pulled out of her bag a burnt crinkled passport.

Lisa burst into a snorting fit. "I'm guessing I shouldn't laugh."

"It's my husband's passport. I put it in the toaster."

"Why would you do that!?"

"We were having a row about who gets what. I said he should keep the jeep, he started shouting I should keep the jeep, then he kept diverting my calls then I saw his passport on the kitchen side and – I didn't think it would catch fire, but it just went whoosh and exploded!"

"People argue about who gets to *take* what, not who gets to *give* what," said Lisa, with a twang of jealousy. How lucky was she, to have a man like *him*. It grieved her to admit it but she had to be honest. "I don't think you two should be splitting up."

"I gave him an ultimatum, me or the Bexley account, and he chose the latter."

"Oh-kay," Lisa drawled. "I'm guessing that's a problem."

"Kate Bexley's the problem, she's five years younger than me, blonde, beautiful, and a multi-millionairess."

"You're beautiful," Lisa cut-in. "And I'm not being funny but, you're minted, he can't be after her money."

"Exactly, I'm from Marshfield, she's from stock like him. I know she fancies him she's obsessed, insisting they have a golf weekend before Monday's meeting, makes me sick, he wants the deal so he's over a barrel. I can't compete, I'm fifty this September."

***

Richard was in dire need of comfort, in the shape of a hot chocolate, whipped cream and marshmallows. He wasn't as bad as Gary but the Hardman foodie gene was definitely a thing. The queue at Café Olé was almost out the door but standing there like a sardine was infinitely better than dealing with non-stop B&B enquiries.

***

"Jeez, and I thought I was insecure," Lisa raised her eyebrows.

"Fact." Liz shrugged her shoulders. "He choose her over me. So I've filed for a divorce."

"Yes but – for the business, not love."

"Since I lost the baby we've drifted apart, we love each other but we're not *in* love, we're just good friends, and to be honest I'm bored."

"Is that why you went on a date with you know

who," grilled nosey Lisa.

"He told me it was an office do!"

"Office do for two." Lisa winked, sassily.

"Ugh, don't, what a sleaze, he kept putting his hand on my leg and I'm trying to save some money on the house sale so I kind of went along with it."

Lisa giggled. "What's he like, Richard Hardman."

***

Richard's ears pricked up at the mention of his name. He glanced over his shoulder and saw Liz Buckley. He just happened to be standing in the queue right next to her table and she was talking to – Lisa? Weird, he never knew they were acquainted but hey; village life for you.

"Sorry, I shouldn't laugh, back to your point, you were saying, about you being just good friends." Richard overheard Lisa say, it was obvious who they were talking about.

"We are, we're *really* good friends." Liz sighed.

"But that's a good starting point, you can build on that."

"Maybe, but where do I start?"

Richard could feel his head swelling.

"Surprise him."

"Surprise him?"

"Yeah, be sexy, you know, be spontaneous."

"You're right, what have I got to lose, I'm going to do it. I'm going to seduce him."

Right at the crucial moment Richard's phone rang. Fumbling to get it out of his pocket he started backing away, praying they wouldn't see him, too late, the ladies turned around.

Startled, Liz spat her coffee out. "Oh, Richard, hello."

"Got to go, urgent message, chow." Richard made a hasty exit out of the cafe.

***

Liz dropped her head into her hands. "Did you see his reaction? He must have heard me say those terrible things about him, and he's coming to value the house Monday, I can't bear the shame, I'll have to say something."

"I'm sorry, I shouldn't laugh," said Lisa, snorting her head off. "I bet he thought he was well in there – until now."

***

Eeny-meeny-miny-moe the one with the hips had to go. Richard performed a little dance as walked through the office door. "Alright, Danny boy?"

"Blimey, what did they put in your hot chocolate?"

"Let's just say I'm in there, big time, actually I'm more than in there, Liz just declared her undying love for me."

"What? After one date!"

***

Lisa couldn't get over it, Liz was really nice, for a rich bitch, and she offered her a weekend job mucking out her horses, and said she could bring Joe, wouldn't that be interesting. Feeling on top of the world, she sauntered into the office of H&C.

"Hi Rodders, where's Lucy? She texted me asking me to pop in, said it was important."

"She's in the kitchen making tea."

"Look after him." She let go of Joe's hand who sprinted over to Nigel's desk and started messing with his files.

"Don't touch that sonny," scowled the un-child-friendly, Rodney.

Joe pointed his gun at him. "My names not Sonny."

Lisa chuckled. "Just give him a pen Rod, he's bored."

Rodney grabbed a piece of paper and a pen out of his pot and handed it to Joe. "Do you want to draw something?" he tried.

"What shall I draw?"

"I've got no idea."

"You draw something," pleaded Joe.

"I don't know what to draw either."

"You're boring," Joe scowled.

"Draw the smart car Rod, easy, a blob with four circles, or your moped, even easier, a line with two circles, be nice to uncle Rod Joe, I'll be back in a minute."

Lisa nipped into the kitchen and saw the open tombola and screwed up bits of paper on the side. She also noticed Lucy seemed cross, uh-oh, so that's what this was all about.

"Lucy, I can explain," blurted Lisa, wondering how.

"You can explain to Nigel when he gets back."

Lisa pushed the kitchen door to. "Lucy, don't say anything, I beg you, you don't understand."

"Too right I don't! Have you ever worked a Saturday?"

"It's Joe. I've got no one to look after him. It's such a struggle, I can't afford a minder, my mum and dad used to look after him, but it's so hard now they've gone."

Lucy looked mortified. "Lisa, I'm so sorry, I feel really bad now, I won't say a word to Nigel, or Gary. I had no idea your parents were dead." She threw her arms around Lisa and gave her a bear hug.

Who said anything about dead? Oh well, whatever-

Trevor, it worked.

"Help!" shouted Rodney.

Lisa and Lucy rushed into the office. Joe was poking his toy gun in Rodney's chest.

"You're not going to shoot me are you?" Rodney held his arms up in mock surrender.

"No, it's plastic, silly." Joe pulled a face.

"He's quite bright you know Rod," Lisa intervened.

"Oh my god, he's *too* cute, look at those big eyes, love him," gushed Lucy.

"When he's not being a pest." Lisa rolled her eyes.

"Mummy look what he drew." Joe held up a phallic looking picture. Lisa and Lucy giggled.

"What? It's Twiki," Rodney frowned. "*Buck Rogers in the 25th Century*, my favourite show."

"Right pest, we've got to go and water nana's plants – on her headstone." Lisa grinned.

"Lisa wait, I'll walk to your car with you, I'm going to the shop to get *Hello*."

"You don't read that rubbish?" Rodney looked surprised.

"Yeah, I love celebrities, they're lush."

"I'll wait here," Lisa offered, "Gary will go nuts if there's only one person in the office."

***

Nigel walked up the stone steps of the old stately home now converted into a retirement home. He knocked gently on the door and peered his head around. There she was, his sweet little mum, sitting in her reclining chair, staring into space.

"Hello Mum," whispered Nigel, kissing her on the head and sitting in the chair beside her.

"Oh it's you," she beamed.

"Yes Mum, it's me," he smiled.

"It's lovely to see you Bob."

"Mum, it's me, Nigel, your son, remember?"

"You're not Bob? You look like Bob."

"Dad's been gone a long time mum."

"Gone? Where?"

"He's sky high, mum."

"Who's a skiver? Not my Bob, he's at Billingsgate, stinks of fish but he aint no skiver."

"Mum you need your hearing aid, why haven't you got it in?"

She pushed the button on her chair until the seat tilted upright then scrutinised his face. "Nigel? Is that you love?"

"Yes Mum, it's me." Nigel felt a glow, it made him so happy when she remembered him.

"What have you done with my hearing aid?"

"It's here look, stuffed down the side of your chair." Nigel pulled it out and replaced the batteries.

"Do you want to help me do the crossword, love?" she asked him.

"I'd love to," Nigel gleamed, placing the hearing aid gently into her ear.

"Ooh dear, don't shout Nigel!" she shouted.

Nigel laughed and turned the volume down. "Have a look in there, for the code word, you like those." He handed her the newspaper.

"I don't want that, where's the Daily Mail, have you put it somewhere, Bob?"

"No, Mum," stated Nigel, authoritively. He handed her the other paper.

"I need a pen, what have you done with my Nigel's pen?"

"I haven't done anything Mum, look it's here, on your chair you were sitting on it."

"What? I can't hear a bleeding thing, I need a new battery." She pointed at the coffee table.

Nigel rummaged through the clutter on the coffee table trying to appease her, knowing full well what was coming next. She would say, *is it there* and he would say, *no Mum, I've already changed it,* and she would say...

"No, you haven't, Bob."

And there it was. Same old, same old. Nigel's patience was wearing thin. "Mum, who do you reckon has the better memory? You or me? And I'm not fricking Bob!"

Defeated, she hit the button and reclined her chair back. Bless her, she was so confused, Nigel felt guilty now, such a rollercoaster of emotion.

The door creaked open, in walked the carer carrying a tray of tea and biscuits. "Hello Flo, tea time, oh hello Nigel, Flo, do you want salad or veg with your scampi later?"

"I don't want none of that bleeding green stuff and I only want four chips," she grimaced. "Do you want me to pay now? Nigel where's my purse? You had it didn't you?"

"You don't need your purse Mum," Nigel sighed.

"If you want anything, do it yourself," she tutted, hitting the forward tilt button on her chair.

The carer put the tray down and walked away Nigel followed her. "Listen, about Mum, she seems more confused lately."

"She seems happy to me." The carer nodded towards his mum and scurried out of the door.

Nigel's mum was smiling, unaware her finger was still on the forward tilt button. "Mum!" He rushed over and managed to catch her just as she was about to fall out onto the floor. She beamed at him, happy, oblivious to the danger, in a world of her own.

"Oh Mum, I hate leaving you here, it's not safe. As soon as I sell the Clunes manor house I'll get out of the flat and buy us a house with a lovely garden. I'll look after you Mum."

He gave his mum a hug, and a tear rolled down his face.

CHAPTER SIX

BENEDICT MYCOCK

Lucy was back from the shops, educating her new best friend Joe as to who was who in *Hello* magazine. A perfect opportunity for Lisa to slink off into kitchen. At least being here, she was kind of working, might help with the tombola scandal. She swiped her phone to call Dan, she couldn't wait to tell him all the stuff she wasn't supposed to tell him about Liz Buckley. It rang and it rang.

"Doo-be-doo-be-doo." Rod skedaddled his way into the kitchen. "Not much excitement going on here today, one more cup of tea, then shut up shop me thinks."

"Really, Rod?" Lisa raised her eyebrows.

"It's almost two, and Nigel did say," suggested a slightly worried Rodney.

"Yeah but you know what a stickler Gary is, I mean, I'm not officially here today Rod, so I *could* turn a blind eye – as long as you don't mention about the tombola," she grinned.

The door ding-a-ling interrupted them. Lisa spied through the doorway, a well-known face walked in. Who was that? Someone she went to school with? Wait a minute, she knew exactly who it was. It was that *really* famous bloke, what's-his-face. The man wandered over to the property board and started browsing. Lisa peeped her head around the door.

"Psst," she whispered, attempting to get Lucy's attention.

Lucy looked up from her magazine, Lisa nodded discreetly toward the mystery visitor. As soon as Lucy saw him her face was a picture – literally, it morphed into *The Scream* painting. She manoeuvred out of her chair, grabbed Joe and crept backwards into the kitchen.

"Oh my God. Oh my God." Lucy was beside herself, her oh-my-God's, were in overdrive. "There's a celebrity out there! A chef I think, quick, what's the name of a famous chef?"

"Alan Titchmarsh?" Rodney guessed.

"He's not a chef." Lisa rolled her eyes.

"He does the weather."

"I've got it!" Lucy cried. "Gordon Ramsey! Oh my God I don't believe it, Gordon Ramsey's in here, I'm going to wet myself, I'm so nervous what are we going to do?"

Lisa stifled a giggle. What a pair of plonkers they were, whoever he was, it definitely wasn't Gordon Ramsay, but she had no plans to tell them that.

"We can't hide in here all day, we have to do something?" Rodney turned to Lisa.

"Don't look at me." She raised her eyebrows. "I'm not officially here today."

"Oh dear, yes, of course," sighed Rodney, "Lucy, you go, keep him talking."

"You go and keep him talking, Rodney!" Lucy retorted.

"What if he asks me a question and I can't answer it? Then what do I do?"

Lisa poked her head around door, the famous bloke was still browsing. "Right," she suggested, "you need to call Nigel."

"He's visiting his mother in Oxbridge," announced Rodney.

"Well done Rodney, you remembered something!" Lucy exclaimed.

"I did." Rodney looked pleased with himself. "I'll

phone Gary he's at home today he told me to call if we need anything." He took his phone out of his pocket and stared at it.

Lisa snatched it off him. "Hey Siri – call Gary." She handed it back. "I hope you realise I did that out of love, I'm not being paid for this crap. Lucy, go and speak to him before he goes."

"What shall I say?" Lucy threw her arms into the air.

"Um – hello?" replied a sarcastic Lisa.

"I can't do that." Lucy was horrified.

"Why not I thought you liked celebrities?" added Rodney.

"I do, oh sod it, alright then, just let me calm down a bit first."

Lucy fanned herself with both hands, took a deep breath then calmly stepped over Joe who had fallen asleep on the kitchen floor and walked back into the office. This should be a laugh.

"Okay Gary, thank you, see you shortly." Rodney cut the call.

"Well?" Lisa grilled him.

"Well what?" asked Rodney, dumbfounded.

Lisa adopted a condescending tone as if she were talking to Joe. "What. Did. Ga-ry. Say."

"Oh, I see, he said, *he may be Gordon Ramsey but he's*

only human, break the ice, make him a coffee but don't make normal coffee, go to Café Olé, it's free today."

"Bad idea, the queues out the door, what else?"

"What else what?"

"Did. He. Say. Any. Thing. Else."

"Oh I see, yes, he said, *tell the old bugger I'll be there in five, have a joke with him, it's best to act normal."*

"So, act normal, go and offer him a *normal* coffee Rod."

Lisa spied through the crack in the door. Lucy was sat at her desk with her head cocked, twiddling her hair, pouting and ogling the Z-list celebrity sitting opposite her browsing property brochures.

"You're right, I'll offer him a normal coffee," declared Rodney, standing there like a lemon. Lisa's patience evaporated. She shoved him through the door and into the limelight. "Right you old bugger one lump or two?" blurted Rodney, rubbing his hands together.

The celebrity looked up. "Are you talking to me?"

"No!" Lucy butted in. "He was talking to me, office banter, how many times do I have to tell you Rodney, it's one, you old bugger," she fake-laughed. "Would you like a coffee, sir?"

Time to leave, before she burst into an uncontrollable snorting fit. Lisa grabbed sleeping Joe, made a hasty exit out of the back door and left them all to it.

***

Gary breezed through the front door, full of beans. "Oi you! F. Off out of my kitchen."

The celebrity sprang out of his chair and turned around. Gary's smile dropped at the realisation he was talking to the lesser spotted local famous person, Ben My-thingamajig.

"Are you talking to me?" He looked at Gary in a confrontational way. "He calls me an old bugger," he pointed at Rodney. "Now you're telling me to F. off, what sort of a buffoon outfit is this?"

Gary strode towards him with his hand outstretched. "I'm so sorry, I thought you were Gordon Ramsey."

"Do I look like Gordon Ramsey?!" he shouted, ignoring Gary's hand.

"Not at all! I'm not saying you look like him, I thought you *were* him," back-peddling Gary, lowered his hand.

"That was my fault," admitted a sheepish Rodney.

"Why does everyone think I'm Gordon Ramsey? Isn't the spiky hair and thick-rimmed glasses a dead giveaway?"

"Yes of course," fibbed Gary, wanting the ground to swallow him up.

"You don't know who I am, do you?" He folded his arms across his chest.

"Of course I do, you're Ben My – um," Gary faltered, "My – um," he knew it, he just didn't want to say *that word* and upset him further.

"Cock!" Lucy yelled. "Mycock, here's a picture of you in here." She proudly held up the magazine.

Gobsmacked Gary glowed red as a beetroot. The celebrity shook his head wearily and threw his arms in the air. "Just call me Ben."

Seeing signs of defeat Gary jumped all over it. He placed an arm around the celebrity's shoulder and escorted him to his desk. "Come and sit here Ben, I'll take your details," he said, his jaw-dropping as he noted his current address. "You're wanting to move?"

"No I just popped in for a loaf of bread, of course I am. I want a bigger house."

"Bit of a tall order." Gary frowned. "There's only two houses bigger than yours around here and none of them are for sale."

"Can't you find me anything?" Seemingly bored, Ben got up and walked over to the window.

"Ooh I've found something!" Gary had to say that – to stop the curse of Brangwin. Ben came away from the window and sat back down. "Nope, sorry, that one's sold already."

"What? In the last two seconds?"

"To be honest with you that's how it is these days with the internet." Gary continued pretending to search.

Ben took his glasses off, rubbed the bridge of his nose and sighed. "Stupid glasses, really piss me off, and they're heavy, do you know I only wore them for a joke for some kids in need thing, now I have to wear them all the time, they're part of my *image*, apparently."

"Here's one. Huge lounge, study, four beds," Gary lied. "Ah, no, sorry, kitchens too small."

Ben perked up. "Sounds perfect."

"You need a house with a big kitchen don't you?"

"Are you having a laugh? Do you think I want to cook after I've been cooking all day?"

"Of course not, I was jesting, Heston – I mean Ben." Gary waved his hand dismissively.

"Honestly mate, Harry isn't it?

"It's Gary," he glanced down at his broken name badge and sighed, "with an R."

"Ha, you've got a stupid surname too, I've never heard of Withenar." Ben winked. "Listen Barry, I'm a takeaway sort of bloke, you know? Why would I cook when there are four Indian restaurants in this village, a Chinese, and a kebab shop, what is the point?"

"Absolutely Benjamin," cheesy-grinned Gary, like they were the best friends.

"Benedict, actually." The not-so famous one corrected him, with a frown.

***

It was getting dark as Lisa drove back from Milton Keynes. She'd nearly forgot to water her parent's plants because she'd hung around at the stupid office all day. Her mum would flip if anything happened to her precious Venus Fly traps. Still, almost home. Pulling up at the junction in Willow Dean she noticed a commotion going on at the manor house opposite. She wiped the windscreen, the police were cordoning it off with tape and forensics were combing the area with torches. Lisa squinted, she could just about make out a huge lump on the ground. One of the forensics shone a light. Crikey, it was a body – a fat man, lying next to the hedge! Lisa shuddered, as she watched one of them bend down and with a gloved hand, pick up what looked like an orange and carefully place it in a clear plastic bag. The sound of a car horn behind startled her. Lisa stuck two fingers up in her rear-view mirror and drove away.

***

Nine am Monday morning and *still* no answer from cowboy outfit BPFS. Gary sat in the smart car drumming his fingers on the dashboard, racking his brains what to do. He'd have to ring Mr Buckley and somehow sneakily find out what time he was back from London. Hopefully Gary could get his smart car retrieved before he did anything stupid with it. Plucking up the courage he called him. It went straight to answer machine. Drat.

Gary closed the back door quietly and loitered in the kitchen spying. Everyone was gathered around in the office singing happy birthday to Nigel. Shit, he'd forgotten. He waited for them to get to the end part then bounded into the office with a huge smile on his face.

"Hip, hip!" he roared.

"Hooray!" sang Lucy and Rodney in unison.

"Replacement!" shouted Lisa, snorting with laughter at her own joke.

"Oi you, less of the cheek." Nigel couldn't help but laugh too. "Life begins at forty I'll have you know, young lady."

"Especially if you're a forty-year-old virgin," quipped Lisa.

Everyone roared, even Gary, as he picked up a handful of envelopes off the mat and handed them all to Nigel. One of them, a jiffy bag, Nigel handed back to Gary.

"Ooh, it's like I'm a birthday boy too." Grinned Gary, opening it. He tipped the contents onto his desk, lots of letters fell out.

"At least your R's problem has cleared up." Nigel dirty laughed.

"Yeah but he's got a problem with his eyes," Lisa pointed to her badge, the letter 'I' had fallen off. Nigel looked down and noticed his 'I' was hanging off.

"I'm fed up with these incompetent companies, MFI whatever their stupid name is – still haven't retrieved my car," Gary huffed. "Right, chop-chop, I'm out of here, work to be done, there's two bottles of bubbly in the fridge so we can celebrate later if you're all good."

***

Lisa pushed Dan against the wheelie bin and snogged him hard, his phone did a half *cock-a-doodle* and they stopped abruptly. Dan took his phone out of his pocket and shook it.

"I think my cocks broken."

Lisa sighed. "I can't believe she thinks my parents are dead."

"Maybe it's the battery."

"When I said my parents have gone, I meant to Milton Keynes, not dead."

"I hope it's the battery, cost me a fortune this phone."

"You haven't been listening to a word I've said have you? Dan this is important!"

"Sorry babe, what did you say?"

"What am I going to do when Miss Marple finds out my parents aren't dead? She'll grass me up about the tombola I know she will. I was right not to like her in the first place, then I liked her, and now I don't like her again. What am I going to do?"

"Find something out about her, like a secret."

"Dan, miss goody two shoes doesn't have any secrets."

***

Gary was sitting in the smart car talking to Mr Buckley, attempting to slyly wheedle information out of him regarding his whereabouts. "We could meet up when you're back, this evening, perhaps?"

"This afternoon would suit me. I'm on route and I really need to talk to you about this sale."

Damn it. He was already heading back and Gary still hadn't managed to get hold of BPFS. "No problem at all Mr Buckley," said Gary, biting his knuckles.

"I shouldn't be too long, relieved to have this wretched Bexley business out of my hair."

"Did you say Bexley – as in Bexley Holdings?" Gary tentatively enquired.

"I did, why, do you know them?"

"I've had unfortunate dealings with that ghastly Kate woman," Gary blurted. "Oops, client confidentiality, I *really* shouldn't have told you that," he cringed.

"No you *really* should have. Tell me more?"

"I don't want to speak out of turn but she sexually harassed my brother, he was only sixteen, poor kid he was doing work experience at the London branch of Brangwin at the time."

"Really? That's interesting, I may need you as a character reference."

"Oh dear, what happened? Let me guess, it had something to do with sex?"

Mr Buckley explained. He'd finished breakfast, opened his briefcase, got the lap top out ready to start work, next thing he knew Kate Bexley had appeared in a dressing gown and thrust her cleavage in his face.

"Because she's a sex-pest," Gary stated, matter-of-fact.

"I tried to crack on but she was adamant, suggesting we have another round of golf, or do something more physical. I said, *we've played golf, I've been riding with you, we've been shooting, been for a swim, it's starting to feel a bit like it's a knockout here.*"

"Doesn't give up until she gets what she wants that one."

"Tell me about it! I said to her, *it's been nice but we have to press on, we've got a tiresome agenda to get through and I have to get back,* and she said, *everything you need is right here* dropped her dressing gown on the floor and was wearing nothing but a bloody birthday suit!"

"Doesn't surprise me, she broke my brother's heart, made him perform every position in the *Karma Sutra*, he thought she loved him, the poor kid. He was too young to understand she was just a female praying mantis."

"She bloody is! I said, *look Kate, we are singing from different song sheets here, I'm a married man and I adore my wife, the deals off* and I drove away with her hanging on to the door handle like a deranged –"

"Bunny boiler?"

"Exactly that. She just stood there, stark bollock naked, and I could see her, in my rear-view mirror, ringing me repeatedly, my phone was buzzing like mad."

"If there's anything I can do to help? Anything at all, Mr Buckley."

"As before, I may need you as a character reference Gary, but let's keep this between you and me for now, the last thing I need is her causing trouble with my wife."

"Absolutely, no problem at all."

Gary smiled inwardly. It's not what you know, it's who you know. The smart car being stuck in his field was the least of Mr Buckley's worries. They had bonded. The deal was in the bag.

***

Richard was busy straightening his desk papers, that way, then this way – no, that way was definitely better – or was it. He really didn't have time for this. Luckily, Dan walked back in.

"Ah, there you are Dandini, what have you been up to?" he quizzed, whilst lint rolling the arms of his suit.

"Nothing." Dan shrugged his shoulders.

"Where do you keep disappearing to?"

"Nowhere."

"Good, now you've finished doing nothing in the land of nowhere, I've got to nip home and have a shower, maybe I should have two," he pondered, "it is a very special day."

"It is?"

"Yeah baby, Liz wants to see me. By the way, they've sorted the B&B issue so that should be the end of those cretinous phone calls."

"And are you going to see her as a client, or?"

"A lover? I certainly am Danny boy. The time has come to consummate our relationship." Richard grabbed his keys then hesitated. "Does my suit look okay, any stray hairs, any fluff?"

***

"This relationship is getting far too serious," Lisa giggled. Ten minutes after their last kissing session and here she was, back behind the wheelie bins at Dan's insistence. "So, what's so important, this, perhaps?" Lisa threw her arms around Dan and started snogging him.

He kissed her briefly then pulled away. "I've got to be quick Lis. I just had to tell you about Rich."

"What about him?"

"He's shagging Liz Buckley."

"What are you talking about?"

"He is! His OCD's in overdrive, he's going round there to give her one, today!"

"No, he isn't." Lisa laughed. "She's been stringing him along to get a good deal that's all. I met up with her in Café Olé she told me everything."

"And you believe her?"

"She's a nice woman Dan, she miscarried four years ago, a little boy, and had to have an emergency hysterectomy, she still can't bring herself to redecorate the nursery, it's so sad. I felt really bad – I mean, sorry for her. I know for a fact Richards talking out of his arse."

"Lis, I heard them the phone, talking about marriage and everything, he even said; *I love you too but no-one must find out about us yet,* it was definitely her."

"Are you kidding me?"

"No babe, she's been stringing you along, she's hardly going to admit it is she? She's a married woman."

Making good use of her lunch break Lisa pulled up in the usual once a month spot, the car park round the back of Burkes End services. She sat in the car staring at the lake, pondering whether to say anything or not. She watched the mandarin ducks dunking their heads underwater, maybe it was a sign, to keep her mouth shut. Two minutes later a black 4x4 with tinted windows pulled up. Lisa got out of the car, walked over to the jeep and climbed into the passenger seat. Oliver Buckley handed her a brown envelope.

"How is he?" he asked.

"Fine."

"Good."

"I bumped into your wife in Café Olé," said Lisa, breaking the uncomfortable one-word atmosphere. "We got talking, she told me all about your little boy, I'm really sorry, Olly."

"You spoke to my wife!" he flashed his eyes angrily.

"It wasn't like that!" Lisa cried.

"If you tell her, you will *never* see me again, understand. I won't give you another penny. It was a mistake Lisa, we were both drunk, it should never have happened. Joe is a mistake!"

Lisa glared daggers at him. "Arsehole." She jumped out of the car, slammed the door as hard as she could and sobbed all the way back to the office.

CHAPTER SEVEN

DAMAGED GOODS

Lisa crept in the back door to discover Lucy had gone to lunch – phew, just the guys at their desks, they'd never notice she had red puffy eyes. She was about to sit down, until she caught the tail end of Gary's phone conversation.

"Absolutely, no problem at all Mr Buckley, I'll be there within the hour."

Lisa froze. "Be where?"

"Buckley wants to meet me at the house," said Gary, fiddling with his cufflinks. "One can only assume he wants to go ahead with the sale." He grabbed a set of car keys off the hook.

"You can't use my smart car." Nigel was taken aback. "I've got to see the Clunes, I've tried ringing but I can't get an answer, so I'm going around there, in the flesh, push them to sign."

"Ah, so it *is* a smart car now is it? You've changed your tune. BFG should be dropping mine off soon, you can use that, I've got to go otherwise I'll be late."

"But – it's my birthday Gary."

"He's right, birthday boys should always get first choice," Lisa quipped.

"You would say that, you're always on Nigel's side."

The girl who cried wolf, for once in her life Lisa wasn't on Nigel's side, but how she was she going to get Gary to understand that without dropping a bombshell?

"I could take you Gary, on the moped?" Rodney offered.

"You can't!" panicked Lisa. The guys stared at her questioningly. "He um – hasn't got a helmet."

"Oh yes he has." Rodney opened his desk drawer and pulled out a helmet. "I always keep a spare just in case," he half-smiled.

"Alright, it's too dangerous," suggested Lisa, whilst emergency-texting Dan.

"He'll be fine." Nigel waved a hand dismissively.

"You better put some air in that back tyre though Rod."

"Very funny Jasper Carrot, thanks Rod, for being the only one to remember ethical code number six, there's no 'I' in team," scowled Gary.

"Just as well eh," Nigel tapped his name badge.

Lisa used their bickering time wisely and texted Dan; *you have to stop Richard.*

"I better go and warm up Maureen." Rodney grabbed his leather jacket, both helmets and skedaddled off.

"Meet you in the car park Rod, I'm so excited, best birthday present ever eh Nige? The Buckley's *and* the Clunes, pop the cork, I'll be back soon."

And he danced off into the kitchen. Lisa pushed past him and threw herself against the back door like a star fish.

"Lisa? Why are you blocking the door?"

"You can't go."

"What do you mean I can't go?"

"I mean, I can't let you go."

"Oh, I get it, bless your little heart, thanks for your concern sweetheart, but I'll be fine honestly, Rod's a very competent driver – well, on a moped."

"It's not the moped Gary, you can't go because, because…"

"Lisa, I haven't got time to play silly beggars." Gary frowned, pushed her aside and opened the door. She watched helplessly, as he stepped out and closed the door behind him.

"...because your brother is shagging his wife." She slumped against the back door.

Lisa waited until she heard them roar off then flung open the door and raced around the back of the shops. Dan was already there, pacing in and out of the wheelie bins.

"Please tell me you stopped him going around there?" she puffed, out of breath.

"Too late." Dan shook his head. "What's going on Lis?"

"It gets worse, Gary's on his way to meet Olly – I mean, Oliver Buckley at the house, I tried to stop him but he wouldn't listen!"

"It gets worse than worse. I got your text so I tried to call Rich then I heard his phone ringing in his desk drawer, bloody twit, anyway, there were loads of filthy text messages, and guess what? They weren't from Liz."

"Who were they from?"

"Lucy."

"What? Are you kidding me?"

"Nope, they've been sexting ever since she came

into the office to use the copier that day. I checked the dates. He's such an idiot getting himself mixed up in a love triangle."

Everything fell into place. That night at the Adam and Eve when Lucy came back from the toilet, Lisa wondered why her hair was ruffled and she had beard chin. The snidey cow, wait until she told Gary. Hang on a minute, she couldn't tell Gary, because then Lucy would tell Gary about her and Dan. Damn it. Lisa had no choice but to confess to Dan, how Lucy had been snooping and found out about them on Facebook. Lucy had promised not to tell anyone but – how could Lisa trust her now? Knowing she was a dirty little... she was right not to like her in the first place.

"This is such a mess, what are we going to do, Dan?"

"Honestly, I'm starting to think you and me are the only sane people around here."

Having a married man's child – far from sane. Lisa was as bad as the rest of them. "You're right, babe, we are," she lied. Poor Dan, she really hated her guilty secret.

"You know what they say babe, keep your enemies close," he winked.

Lisa snuck in the back door and closed it discreetly. She turned around, guess who was standing there, grinning in her face?

"Wish me luck, I'm off to do my first viewing," said the lying, two-faced, gold-digger.

"Break a leg." Lisa smiled through gritted teeth, closing the door behind her. "Literally."

***

The automatic gates opened. Richard pulled onto the drive in his black Audi sport with his impressive personalised registration number SH4 GGU. He combed his hair in the mirror, smoothed the invisible creases out of his shirt, straightened his tie, picked microscopic fluff off his suit, squirted breath freshener into his mouth and broke wind about four times.

***

Nigel pulled up outside the nuthouse aka the Clunes residence. Just when he thought they couldn't get any weirder, he noticed the entrance was cordoned off with cones and orange and white police tape. He scratched his head and drove slowly past – spooky.

***

Richard knocked on the big oak door. Almost immediately she answered, dressed in her smelly horse clobber. Choosing to ignore Gary's words ringing in his ears; *she'll be covered in hair,* he braced himself. They both attempted to speak at the same time.

"Sorry, after you." Liz chuckled awkwardly. "Ladies first." Richard grinned.

"Look Richard, about the other day, in the coffee shop, the things I said. I'm so sorry, I really am," she said, going all coy.

"Don't apologise, it's no big deal, we both know why I'm here, so let's just get on with it."

"Music to my ears." Liz smiled and sighed with relief. She placed her hand on his shoulder. "You really are a sweet man Richard, come on in."

Get in there. Lady killer Richard sauntered into the house.

"Where would you like to start?" she asked.

"The bedroom?" Richard winked.

"Excellent idea, let's start from the top and work our way down."

Crikey, it was just like Kate, all over again. Richard shrugged his shoulders. "I'm game if you are." He followed her up the stairs like a love-sick puppy.

"Listen, I'm going nip off and to slip into something a little more –"

"Spontaneous? Sexy?"

"I was going to say appropriate actually." She seemed a little uncomfortable, obviously all part of the weird sex game. Kate used to be like that too. "Richard, I'll leave you to it, you know what to do, don't you?"

"I've done this a few times." He grinned.

"Course you have, silly me, I won't be long, back in in a tick."

Probably off to get the handcuffs and that. Richard started undoing his tie.

***

Lisa and Dan were propped up against the wheelie bins, chuffing away like a pair of chimneys, waiting for the apocalypse.

"Hi guys." Ugh, look who it wasn't, Miss Marple. "Mind if I join you?" she *told* them rather than asked, taking a cigarette out of her Louis Vuitton handbag.

The cheek of it. Just because she knew where their secret meeting place was, she thought it was okay to join them did she? Lisa could feel her temperature rising to dangerous levels. She flashed her angry eyes at Dan, he squeezed her arm reassuringly.

"Course you can, we, we're all friends here, not *enemies*," he said, giving Lisa a sly wink.

"Yeah Lisa, and friends don't have secrets, do they?" said Lucy, giving her a bitchy grin.

***

Gary tapped Rodney on the shoulder. "Pull over!" he shouted through his helmet.

He couldn't wait to get off that thing. How anyone could get a kick out of hugging an engine he did not know. He struggled and struggled to get his big head out of the helmet, eventually it popped out like a cork. "I'll walk from here," grumbled Gary, thrusting the helmet into Rodney's chest.

"Are you sure Gary, it's only around the corner?"

"Exactly, I can't be seen on the back of this rust bucket, meet me here in an hour, I don't want to rush Buckley into signing, it's a sensitive deal, needs to be handled professionally."

Rodney gave Gary a wave and drove away just as it started to rain. Gary instantly regretted his decision but luck was on his side, two seconds later a red Porsche pulled up. A tinted window glided down to reveal a grinning, blonde-haired, sunglasses wearing, very rich looking lady. "Excuse me, I'm looking for the Buckley household?"

"How queer, that's exactly where I'm going," uttered a pleasantly surprised Gary.

"Hop in." The kind woman offered.

***

Richard had taken off all his clothes, except for his bright red novelty *Love Doctor* boxer shorts. He sniffed his armpits then slid into the bed under the purple silk duvet, waiting excitedly for the love games to commence.

***

Gravel spewed everywhere as the red Porsche roared onto the drive before screeching to a halt. A bit disrespectful, driving like that. Gary leapt out of the passenger side and saw Richard's Audi. Oliver Buckley pulled up directly behind it and jumped out of his 4x4.

"What the hell is he doing here?" Gary pointed at the Audi.

"What the hell are you doing here?" barked Mr Buckley, extremely vexed.

"We've got an appointment remember?"

"I know that you idiot," Mr Buckley retorted. "What are you doing here, with *her*?"

The Porsche window rolled down the woman smiled at Mr Buckley. "Such a nice welcome."

Gary's hand flew up to his mouth. He thought she'd seemed familiar. It was *her,* a much older Kate Bexley! He suddenly recognised her from one of Richard's old photos.

"If my wife sees you, I'll be in deep trouble, why are you stalking me?" snapped Mr Buckley.

"You really rate yourself, don't you? I only wanted sex get over it." She belittled him.

"Really? You chased me, then you kept ringing my phone, now you've kidnapped my estate agent!"

Gary stood there like a lemon, watching it all unfold.

"Don't flatter yourself old man, you left this behind." She handed him a laptop through the window. "If you hadn't cancelled my call's I wouldn't have had to follow you." The electric window glided back up, the car spun around and roared off kicking up gravel, all over Gary.

A loud scream resonated from inside the house. Mr Buckley raced to the front door Gary lagged behind. He tore up the stairs two at a time, Gary followed – one at a time.

***

"I know your naughty secret," Lucy sniggered.

She couldn't possibly know about Ollie being Joe's father, or could she? She was Miss Marple after all. Lisa gulped nervously. "It's not true."

"I know it isn't. Rodney told me."

"Rodney?" Lisa was confused. "What are you on about?"

"Your parents aren't dead, they're in Milton Keynes."

Lisa's instantaneous relief was immediately quashed by the realisation she'd end up out of a job if Lucy snitched on her. "Don't say anything about the tombola, please," she begged.

"Pinky promise, I'm just happy your parents aren't dead, I felt so bad on you. Hey guys, I'll tell you something funny." She giggled. "Gary Hardman, he's a bit camp isn't he, and Nigel Camp, well, he's a bit of a hard man isn't he."

The three of them stared at each other in disbelief then burst into a laughing fit. Lucy was guffawing at her amazingly funny observation. Lisa and Dan were snorting because she'd only just worked it out.

***

Gary couldn't believe what he was seeing, his brother, in bed, naked. "Richard?"

"Liz?" Mr Buckley looked devastated.

"It was her idea!" Richard exclaimed, jostling with the sheets, scrambling of the bed.

"How dare you! When I said start in the bedroom, I meant measure it, you creep!"

Gary picked up Richards clothes and launched them at his head. "Get dressed, you embarrassing pervert!"

Liz Buckley rushed into her husband's arms. "Olly, I'm so sorry, I've been such a fool, I was so jealous of you and that woman."

"No Liz, I've been a fool, I've cancelled the deal."

"But – it was so important to you?"

"You're more important to me, more than anything else in the world."

"What about the house?"

"The only reason I asked that clown round here was

to tell him the sale is off." He sneered at Gary, then turned back to his wife "I love you Pumpkin."

"Oh Olly-poo, I love you too."

"I've booked us a cruise, just the two of us, to the Seychelles."

"Oh darling, that's perfect, I can't wait. When are we going?"

"We're leaving tonight, so get packing." He grinned. "By the way, I can't seem to find it anywhere, have you seen my passport?"

***

"Lucy we'd better go, it's only us two in the office. Dan come and have a drink."

"I can't, I'm the only one in the office."

"Oh, come on, don't be a party pooper," Lucy teased.

"It's Nigel's birthday, we've got champagne in the fridge." Lisa put her hands in the prayer position. "Please? I think we're all going to need one."

"Alright then, I'll have to be quick though."

They puffed frantically then extinguished their cigarettes.

"Oh my god, I'm so dizzy," muttered Lucy. "I've never smoked a fag that quick."

Good. Hopefully she would faint and they could throw her in the wheelie bin.

***

"It's like a scene from *Gone with the Wind*." Gary gazed lovingly at the Buckley's. "All we need now is some popcorn."

That killed the moment. Mr Buckley flipped. "Get out of my house! As for you, you low-life." He lunged toward Richard and grabbed him by the scruff. Gary's brotherly instinct kicked in, he pulled Buckley off and got a back hander in the face. Seizing the moment, Richard got a hold of his shoes and scrambled for the door, Gary staggered out behind him. As soon as he was safely out of arms reach Gary stopped in the doorway and turned around, blood oozing from his nose.

"Does this mean the deals off? Or –"

"Get out – GAY! Before I set my dogs on you!"

"Oh, and Gary? I've sorted your car problem." Mrs Buckley smiled sweetly then slammed the bedroom door hard, in his face.

***

The amazing power of alcohol. Lisa didn't care a fig about any of it anymore. It wasn't her problem. She, Dan and Lucy were quaffing champagne out of plastic cups, laughing and joking, until Nigel walked in.

"What the bleeding hell's he doing here?"

"Celebrating your birthday, don't be a miserable old fart, have a drink." Lisa handed him a plastic cup.

"Oh, why not, who gives a flying –"

***

"Another mess you've gotten us into. I told you, you're playing with fire, this is all your stupid fault, damaged goods you are," moaned Gary, holding a tissue up to his bloody nose as Richard wheel spun out of the gates.

"You haven't done a bad job of pissing them off yourself." Richard pointed out of the passenger window as he drove past the muddy field. Gary's smart car was being taken away on the back of a big truck bearing the logo; *Same Day Crush*.

***

The dangerous power of alcohol. Loose lips sink ships. Lisa had expected to feel better having blurted to Lucy about Richard and Liz Buckley's affair, instead the sweet taste of revenge had left her feeling a bit sour. She sat hiccoughing, with her arm around Lucy's shoulder while she cried her little welsh heart out. The poor girl was heartbroken.

***

Worst day ever. Dishevelled Richard stumbled into his empty office. Flipping Dandini back in the land of nowhere, doing nothing. The phone rang, Richard snatched up the receiver.

"Good afternoon the B&B Partnership – yes madam, we have several rooms available, en-suite, single or double?"

***

Lisa was leaning against the back door, lost in a sozzled world of love-land, snogging Dan's head off when Gary burst through it, knocking their party hats off.

"What's he doing here?" yelled an angry Gary.

"I'm off, happy birthday Nige!" Dan shouted, as he did a disappearing act.

"Cheers buddy, thanks for coming," called Nigel.

"Gary, why have you got a red nose, estate agents in need?" Lisa stifled a tipsy grin.

"I see, everyone's having a party while this has been one of the worst days of my entire life."

"Cheer up Gazza." Lisa handed him a drink and put her party hat on his head. "Have a drink even Rod's had one."

"Brilliant, so how was he planning on picking me up?"

Rodney entered the kitchen wearing his orange sparkly paper hat and a party whistle dangling out of his mouth. "I've got no idea," he slurred, "haven't got a clue." The party whistle fell out of his mouth and plopped into his paper cup of champagne.

"Oh look, the stripper-grams here." Lisa pointed, noticing a policeman and a policewoman walk through the front door.

"Damn, I forgot to book it. Well done Lisa, at least I can rely on someone around here," Gary grumbled at Rodney.

"I never booked it?" admitted Lisa.

"Who the hell did?" quizzed Gary.

Lisa and Gary stared at each other. Like a scene from a John Wayne film, they swaggered out of the kitchen, side by side, preparing to face the consequences. Meanwhile, nonchalant Lucy was perched on the edge of Nigel's desk guffawing at his corny jokes. Gary and Lisa stared at each other in shocked disbelief as the two officers approached Nigel.

"Are you Nigel Camp?" asked the policewoman.

"For my sins," Nigel winked, playing along.

"We'd like you to accompany us to the station, we have some questions for you."

"Are you going to sing them to me?"

Uh-oh, Nigel was in comedian mode. Somehow Lisa didn't think this was going to be funny.

"No, I am not," said the stern policewoman.

E.A

"Stop wasting my time, are you going to get your kit off or not?" Nigel dirty-laughed.

"Not," the irritated policewoman persisted.

"Oh, I get it, you want me to do this!" Nigel ripped open her shirt revealing a bra.

Oh. My. God. What just happened? Lisa's problems suddenly paled into insignificance.

"Nigel, I don't think –" tried Gary.

"Sorry to burst your bubble Gary," Nigel cut in, "this is my birthday present, not yours."

"Nigel Camp, you have the right to remain silent, anything you do say may be taken down and used as evidence against you," declared the policewoman, buttoning herself back up.

"I think you should get your money back Gazza, these two are shit," Nigel belly-laughed and offered them his wrists.

Gary stared at Lisa his eyes woefully wide, she shrugged her shoulders and looked at Lucy, who turned to Rodney, half-smiling with his distorted wet party whistle still in his mouth.

"You do not have to say anything but it may harm your defence if you do not mention when questioned something you will later rely on in court." The policewoman handcuffed him.

"You really are going all the way, aren't you?" Nigel

chuckled. The policewoman snapped the cuffs shut. "Hang on a minute, these cuffs are real?"

"No shit Sherlock." The policewoman raised her eyebrows. "Nigel Camp, I'm arresting you on suspicion of murdering Cedric Theodore Clunes – oh and sexual assault."

"You can't do that, it's his fortieth birthday!" Gary exclaimed.

"You know what they say," the policewoman smiled sarcastically.

"Life imprisonment begins at forty?" replied the policeman.

The police officers laughed at Nigel's expense.

"I haven't done anything. You've got the wrong man! Tell 'em Gary, I'm innocent!"

"Ethical code number seven." was all Gary had to say on the matter.

"There's no 'I' in team?" guessed Lucy.

"That's ethical code number six." Lisa informed her. "Number seven's – if you get into trouble, you're on your own."

Stone-faced Gary folded his arms across his chest. "Absolutely."

The police officers dragged Nigel away, still wearing his party hat. Rodney, half smiling-half dumbfounded, started clapping and blew his champagne drenched out of tune, party whistle.

~~~

~ WHERE ARE THEY NOW ~

Lisa rubbed her pregnant tummy and sipped her chai tea, flicking through the pages of her wedding album, reminiscing. She smiled fondly at the group photo of her and her husband, surrounding the happy pair; Gary, Nigel, Richard, Lucy, Rodney, little Joe, and the Buckley's. Standing on the beach, carefree, with their bare feet nuzzling in the white sand. What a life-changing year it had been, for all of them...

Nigel was found guilty and sentenced to life imprisonment for the murder of Mr Clunes. It was a cut and dried case, his prints were all over the chainsaw and the orange, mysteriously found next to Mr Clunes head as he lay dead. They were dark times. The company was on the brink of collapse. Lisa knew Nigel was innocent but it was Miss Marple who really came up trumps. Mrs Clunes confessed to Lucy, it was she, who smashed her husband over the head with the chainsaw, repeatedly, which she claimed was to cure his stammering. Mrs Clunes was charged with manslaughter on the grounds of diminished responsibility and sentenced to five years in prison. Nigel was released after six months, during which time his beloved mum passed away. On the plus side, he inherited a fair sum, coupled with the wrongful conviction compensation he was able to turn his life around and buy a big house with a lovely garden and invest in the crumbling H&C business.

Gary, on the other hand, what a nightmare that was. He learned the awful truth about Lindsay at Rodney's retirement do in the Adam and Eve. The drinks were flowing and they decided to play *Truth or Dare*. Lisa would never forget that night. Gary confessed about the office cam and then asked Rodney to finish the iPad story, as to why Lindsay was at the client's house that day. It was only supposed to be a bit of fun, everyone expected Rodney to say; *I don't know,* or *I haven't got a clue,* but to everyone's surprise he told Gary she was prancing around in the bedroom wearing sexy underwear! Heartbroken, Gary confronted Lindsay, she laughed in his face and admitted she'd been having an affair for three years, just like that, and the horrible bitch left him.

And Lucy – well that was just plain weird. She was so devastated to learn of Richard's shenanigans with Liz Buckley, she sought revenge on Richard by confessing about their affair to Gary. It backfired. She was given instant dismissal for breaking all seven of H&C's ethical codes in one go. That's how it came to pass that bored and unemployed Lucy ended up working as a housekeeper for lonely widow Mrs Clunes. They became close and Lucy grew suspicious when she learned how much she despised her husband. All it took was an afternoon of prosecco with Mrs Clunes who had never touched a drop of alcohol in her life, and the truth came out, clever Lucy recorded the confession on her phone and that was it. Her name hit the newspapers and (with the help of her pushy mother) she bounced back and landed herself a dream job as a TV presenter on a property channel. Despite everything, her soft spot for Richard remained.

Talking of Richard, what a scoop that was. Someone put in an anonymous complaint to the B&B Head Office about his behaviour with Liz Buckley. Richard admitted it and was sacked for indecent conduct and banned from working in estate agency. He fell into a deep depression after his OCD increased to unmanageable levels. He lost everything and ended up in a rundown council house riddled with damp. Lucy felt sorry for him, understandably, seeing as it was her that put in the anonymous complaint. She felt so bad she helped him pioneer his own property programme; *Dickie Damp Grants* – helping people claim off the council to repair their properties damaged by dry and wet rot. Local hero Richard became a well-known heartthrob, often featured in regional newspapers surrounded by beautiful women.

As for Lisa, she was heartbroken when Dan left B&B

to work in Milton Keynes following Richard's demise. She threw herself into her job, Gary and Nigel were so impressed that they promoted her to senior negotiator. She continued working with the horses part-time, and became firm friends with Liz Buckley. However, Lisa being Lisa, couldn't live with the guilt and came clean to Liz that Oliver was Joe's father. After the initial anger and shock wore off Liz was over the moon to discover she (sort of) had a son. She hadn't kept that little boy's room intact all these years for nothing. Lisa agreed they could have Joe alternate weekends, and as a thank you, the kind-hearted millionaire couple bought Lisa and Joe a house nearby.

It doesn't end there. Dan was head-hunted from his position in Milton Keynes by Gary and Nigel to become managing director of their newly opened office in Burkes End. It was a fairy tale ending for Lisa and Dan who tied the knot on a beach in Santorini, paid for by the Buckley's with no expense spared. And it was there that Gary met the love of his life – David.

Lucy is now dating a well-known male TV presenter and Gary and Nigel went on to open a further twenty offices and became one of the most successful Estate Agencies in the country.

~~ THE END ~~

THANK YOU!

Oliver Martin – for such a brill cover, as always, I love it ☺ and more importantly, for having the funniest funny bone and helping me create the dialogue.

Marina Sawyer – for spurring me on, believing in my crazy characters and forcing me to share this book which has been sitting in my bottom draw for a while...

Martina Healy – my editing super-hero which she does effortlessly and brilliantly. Thanks for helping me write this 'proper' without mitakes ha ha.

Teri Coffey – my daughter and best friend who sat with me every Friday and helped me plan the story... oh and thanks Teri for the inspiration and the attitude for Lisa's character.

Last but not least – thumbs up to **Joe Coffey** for giving me a Waddley Bottom.

~~~

Printed in Great Britain
by Amazon